T0128098

MEMOIRS OF A MISFIT

MEMOIRS OF A MISFIT

SATISH MALLYA

MEMOIRS OF A MISFIT

iUniverse books may be ordered through booksellers or by contacting:

iUniverse
1663 Liberty Drive
Bloomington, IN 47403
www.iuniverse.com
1-800-Authors (1-800-288-4677)

ISBN: 978-1-4917-6296-7 (sc)
ISBN: 978-1-4917-6295-0 (e)

Library of Congress Control Number: 2015903758

Print information available on the last page.

iUniverse rev. date: 06/12/2015

Dedicated to fond memories
of my loving parents

The initiation

A square peg in a round hole is a popular quote implying a state of existence that is not in harmony with the surrounding reality. The vast majority of humans experience a disconnect with their lives at one time or another which is often resolved through compromise within and through adjustment with external circumstances. The choice between excercising free will on the one hand and yielding to the dictates of destiny on the other, is a difficult one. Personal successes are often attributed to the former while the latter is held responsible for failures. It is certainly convenient to delegate responsibility to another agency for situations that are essentially of one's own making. Life is nothing but a series of experiences, some being the outcomes of conscious efforts while others are the results of circumstances beyond our control. This is the tale of Satyananda Koteswar, a misfit existing in a state of perpetual denial. He was endowed with a split personality to match the fusion of two sanskrit terms, Satya (truth) and Ananda (bliss), given to him as his principal identity. Although in the course of his adult life Satyananda had often heard it said that there is only one universal unchanging truth he had never fully understood its import. From numerous unpleasant experiences very early in life, he had come to realize that at least in his case, speaking the truth seldom resulted in bliss. As a result, he rarely lived up to the spirit implied in the first part of his given name and consequently seemed to be eternally in search of the state of being promised by the latter half. Satyananda was born to Mandakini and Nityananda Koteswar, in a small room in his maternal grand father's home in Bailoor which was then a very small town located in the South Canara district of Karnataka in the southern part of India. Since that eventful day, the town of Bailoor was immortalized in his birth, school and college certificates and ofcourse in numerous editions of his passport. Satyananda had been called upon to explain the location of this place numerous times. Strangely enough, over the course of his life, he had visited Bailoor much less than the number of times he had been asked to describe its geographic location and size. The first cry of a new born is variously interpreted by scholars as a gasp of breath or a painful howl or something to that effect. Spiritual Masters may perhaps opine that the child's first cry is an expression of indignation on being disturbed while in deep communion with the creator. It could very well be that the child is unhappy on being compelled to surrender the comfort and security of the mother's womb only to be ejected into a world of suffering. It appears that even a new born is capable of recognizing an unjust barter. Then again, we are told that the ego does not express itself until the child attains the age of five. If such is the case then the child could not care less whether it is in or out of the mother's womb. Be that as it may, it appears that when Satyananda finally chose to arrive, he did not conform to the law of natural entry. To the extreme discomfort and anxiety of the midwife who delivered him, this baby did not cry at birth. Now, we all know that midwives are most comfortable when there is a lot of hustle, bustle, anxiety, groaning and moaning in the delivery room ending in relief at the climax. This is a moment of glory savoured by medical professionals. They can take credit for what is essentially an act of God. In Satyananda's case however, a silent entry into the world ensured that the midwife earned the credit. Therein lay the genesis for his future life as a social misfit. The seeds of situations that unfolded subsequently in his life were perhaps planted in the delivery room of that obscure house in a very small town. Fortunately for Satyananda the midwife was a level headed individual who preferred to experiment with the therapeutic effects of complementary medicine rather than administering some strong drug into his helpless body. Her treatment was to brand the child with a red hot ember, not once but many times leaving behind corporeal blemishes that served as a constant reminder of an unusual experiment. Later in the journey of life, deeper and more painful scars would be imprinted at the mental and psychological levels as he ventured into alien cultures. He was to experiment with spirituality in an attempt to bring some balance and sanity in his life. Not surprisingly, for the misfit these forays into unknown realms were fraught with challenges.

The Koteswars resided in a rental apartment in Mumbai during Satyananda's early childhood. The neighbourhood was infested with gangs given to settling scores between themselves periodically in their attempts to widen their spheres of influence and expand their nefarious businesses. The income from operating gambling dens and bootlegging illicit country liquor was apparently lucrative enough to sacrifice human lives. The grapevine would faithfully broadcast news on the latest arrest of infamous members and their subsequent release from custody. The soda water bottle containing carbonated drinks was a favoured weapon; the local version of the cluster bomb. Innocent bystanders would often be injured in the cross fire. Having learned to interpret subtle signs of imminent trouble, the occupants of buildings in the neighbourhood were wise enough to keep out of harm's way. There was also the danger that one could be questioned by the police, as a witness to these senseless acts of violence. The consequence of this would be worse than physical injury from flying glass pieces. The members of these gangs were also adept at escalating minor skirmishes to major public unrests. They profited from looting local shops indiscriminately when political and social issues were settled on the streets of Mumbai. Many were shot and even killed when the army was called in to restore normalcy. To their credit, these otherwise ruthless characters had a soft corner for law abiding citizens, especially those who donated generously to the cultural events organized by them during religious festivals.

The family moved to a safer neighbourhood when his hard working parents had saved enough to purchase their own apartment. The apartment complex comprised three large buildings. The paved ground between these edifices was utilized as a parking lot by those who could afford the luxury of owning vehicles. The residents had organized themselves into a cooperative society. In accordance with the rules, periodic meetings of this society were held in the parking lot. A pattern emerged after a number of such meetings had taken place. As the meetings progressed the parking lot would be transformed into a platform for the uninhibited expression of a variety of emotions, particularly those resulting from suppressed anger, jealousy and hatred. A typical meeting would proceed normally, until a particular item on the agenda would evoke strong criticism from one group followed by a sharp rebuttal from the opposite camp. Before long a physical altercation would ensue and the meeting would end abruptly. Everyone's vocubulary of unprintable terminology would be upgraded at each meeting. Needless to say, records of decisions were never maintained since the proceedings were unworthy of being commited to writing. There was seldom any constructive action and matters languished for painfully long periods until they were miraculously resolved on their own. Codes of conduct and etiquette were never put in place since a concensus prior to implementation would be impossible under the circumstances. Although the cooperative society was technically run by volunteers, there were certain perks for those holding positions in the management committee, one among them being kickbacks from tenders for repair work. The potential for profit was the driving force behind the immense competition for positions on this committee. At one time the sitting president of the committee had an entire building painted and the parking lot converted into a temporary marriage hall and kitchen to celebrate her daughter's marriage. It mattered little to her that the residents were put to great inconvenience for several days. Her decision went unchallenged since she was known to unleash her two sons on anyone who dared to so much as whisper a protest. These specimens excelled in exhibiting uncultured behaviour. They were actually donkeys in sheep's clothing, known to either bray or bleat depending on whether they were challenged by superior brawn or brain. They preyed on girls who came to offer prayers at the small temple constructed around a giant sacred *Aswatta* tree in the center of the parking lot. They were observed to frequently coach a mentally challenged boy on novel techniques for harassing girls. The scenes that would unfold as the girls scattered in fright was a constant source of entertainment for them. Their family business specialized in creative accounting, offering advice to a clientele eager to seize any opportunity to launder wealth accumulated through unlawful means. It was rumoured that every male member of this family had been imprisoned for tax evasion at one time or the other. It appears the family was united in this regard and as directors of their company, took turns to admit guilt, own responsibility and spend the requisite time behind bars. Providing equal opportunity to everyone was clearly the honourable thing to do. A family that prays for pardon together stays together.

In stark contrast, the building complex was home to a few pious souls who were ever eager to sponsor spiritual discourses delivered by missionaries and sages. They were conducted in large temporary tents raised on the parking lot. In the midst of a vivid description of the triumph of good over evil, a certain individual residing on the top floor would take the opportunity to project himself as an astute businessman. He would be heard carrying on an animated conversation over the telephone, loud enough to be clearly audible to the gathering several storeys below. There was a general tendency to believe at first, that this was an isolated incident attributable to coincidence. However the audience did not fail to notice an emerging pattern in the repeated synchronization of telephonic conversations with the timings of these religious meetings. These conversations would essentially entail instructions for the participant at the other end of the line, to deliver a large sum of money to this gentleman at their next meeting. Patience was wearing thin and it was felt that drastic action was essential to curb this repeated nuisance. Someone hit upon a devious plan to teach this individual a well deserved lesson. Unbenownst to this vane exhibitionist, the proceedings of the spiritual meetings were recorded. To everyone's amusement, it was discovered that this gentleman's frequent conversations were now captured on tape. This information was leaked to the revenue and taxation department and shortly thereafter our friend had an unwelcome visitor from the civil service to whom he was compelled to explain his business dealings. The booming voice was now replaced by a whimper. Even so, some determined evesdroppers heard him explain to an unconvinced auditor, that these were one sided conversations between him and a non existent party at the other end; the sole purpose being to impress his neighbours. News travelling through the grapevine hinted at a princely settlement which this actor could scarcely afford. He had to dig deep in his pockets to pay for a shallow attempt to gain recognition for a non existent acumen in business matters.

The womenfolk from families residing on the upper floors of the buildings had devised a novel technique for saving time and at the same time avoiding exertion from using the stairway. A basket tied to a long rope would be lowered to the ground, where a hawker would be waiting patiently, to retrieve the money placed inside and replace it with the desired produce and the change. Obesity was an unfortunate consequence of this innovation. What could have been an opportunity for inexpensive physical exercise was sacrificed in the interest of laziness. Saving time through intelligent management was hardly a valid excuse for those who had a lot of spare time on their hands. Domestic servants made certain that any remaining avenues for exercise were closed to these individuals. In addition to performing all household chores they also made frequent trips for procuring essential items for which a home delivery service was unavailable. Since many residents had made fortunes through dubious means, their children were also recepients of generous sums as pocket money. This placed the other children at a disadvantage when participating in activities that involved financial contributions. Satyananda's father was an honest hardworking family man who believed in providing for basic necessities. He was disinclined to encourage any activity that involved unnecessary expenditure. Consequently, from a very young age it was an unspoken agreement between his father and Satyananda that he would not be entitled to receive any spending money. He was expected to make a case when in dire need and the final outcome was left to the discretion of his father. There was no expectation that his father would justify any decisions that were not in Satyananda's favour. He had no objection to such an arrangement since he had no particular desire to indulge in any activities that involved monetary expenditure. Nonetheless, at times he felt despondent when explaining his situation to friends from well to do backgrounds. Predictably their standard response was to exclude him from such activities except when his skills were in demand such as at cricket matches. He was a star performer on the team.

When he attained the requiste age for attending elementary school, his father enrolled him in a semi private school in Mumbai. The opening day of school marked a significant milestone in young Satyananda's life as it was the first among many occasions when he wet his pants. Being introverted, the anxiety of having to mingle with strangers must have taken its toll. When nature knocked with increasing urgency as time progressed, he was too timid to ask the teacher to be excused in order to answer its call. The fact that the washroom was located in the realm of the unknown must have weighed heavily on his mind since he had a morbid fear of the dark. He was willing to do anything in his power to postpone a visit to that place. Fortunately for him, emptying his bladder coincided with the ringing of the bell announcing recess. There he was! Seated in the first row, watching the urine meander through the crevices in the floor with mixed emotions of horror and relief until its progress was finally halted by the wall. Saved by the bell, he sat there through recess hoping that his misadventure would go unnoticed. Thus it came to pass that our budding hero was destined to be initiated into the Indian education system, through a trial by uric acid. Another milestone was achieved at the end of the first trimester when he found himself at the bottom of the class in scholastic standing. As a consequence, he was previleged to be introduced to two fundamental lessons that had far reaching implications in his life. First, he learned that it was extremely important to do well in school and secondly it was wise to approach his father only if he had a good report card. As far as Nityananda Koteswar was concerned, this piece of paper was the only meaningful evidence of the diligence of the student. The senior had no hesitation in expressing his disappointment at junior's performance. It was imperative that the chip be appropriately initiated into the old block's way of thinking. After a cursory look at the dismal report card, the wise one quietly slipped his hand under the initiate's shorts, pinched his thigh and launched him into orbit. This techique went by the coloquial term *jhangulli*, which when translated essentially means tickling the thighs. Far from being a pleasant sensation, it is an experience that no self respecting man would wish to place on his resume. Some experiences are etched in memory only when they are never repeated. The inaugural event was more than adequate for Satyananda to guage his father's expertise at this silent yet deadly technique. The effect was so profound that he voluntarily opted to be a model student during his entire educational career. Such is the power of the paternal touch! Thus it was not surprising that, in the third grade he was awarded a merit certificate for good conduct and application. Personally, he was not convinced that his conduct was exemplary as proclaimed by this testimonial. Indeed, he could be prone to covert misbehaviour when confronted with situations that were not to his liking.

On one occasion the class teacher had no choice but to distance Satyananda from his peers for their own well being. It so happened that much against his wishes, he was selected for a part in a group dance to be performed at the annual talent show. After several failed attempts to discretely make it known that he was not too keen on participation, he hit upon a plan that was devious by design, pregnant with possibilities and simple to execute. With music playing in the background, participants were required to hold hands to form a large circle and subsequently raise their hands to converge into a small circle. The former sequence was meant to depict a lotus opening its petals to welcome the rising sun and the latter to signify the closing of petals at sunset. As the boys converged to herald the night, dark thoughts would cloud the mind of a certain eight year old, prompting him to place a well timed kick on the foot of a fellow student on the opposite side. At first, it was only a soft exploratory tap on the lower half of the victim's leg. When it went largely unnoticed, in subsequent rehearsals, he gradually increased the force of the kicks while at the same time targetting the thigh. This brotherly act brought forth a protest, mild at first but with increasing intensity and pitch commensurate with the force behind each delivery. At first, the teacher chose to ignore the protests refusing to accept that Satyananda could be capable of aggression. On the contrary, she preferred to change the other boy's position rather than question Satyananda's alleged misconduct. The next eposide of this drama was punctuated with a loud scream that pierced the very core of Satyananda's being. Sadly, he had misjudged the height and his kick had landed on a rather delicate part of the other boy's anatomy. The teacher had not failed to notice the horror and guilt reflected on Satyananda's face. His role was abruptly withdrawn marking the end of his dancing exploits. Alas, the recepient of the merit certificate for good conduct had not lived up to the spirit of the award. Needless to say, the turn of events were entirely to his satisfaction.

The headmaster was a diehard from the then old school, always attired in an impeccably designed suit with an english accent to match. This perpetually eligible elderly bachelor exhibited a flair for dramatics. While delivering animated lectures on english literary works, he would often indulge in role play, emerging from behind the cupboard brandishing a sword or bending down on his knees to peep through the keyhole in the door. Teachers of vernacular subjects were in a class by themselves. One such exhibited a chronic obsession with his own past and would often digress from the topic under discussion in order to reminisce on the good old days spent in his ancestral village. At the best of times it was difficult to separate fact from fiction, myth from hallucination, antecedent from subsequent. While superimposing the qualities of a super human being on his own personality, he would unabashedly indulge in self praise even as he made a show of humility. If he was to be believed, on many a memorable occasion, he had apparently pinned the village wrestling champion on the mat in a manner that the hapless champion was compelled to beg for mercy. Why the oft-defeated individual continued to hold the title of a champion remained unclear to everyone. Ofcourse none dared to demand clarification. The social sciences teacher was in the habit of snorting snuff at frequent intervals. He would extol the virtues of personal and collective hygiene while giving vent to sporadic bouts of uncontrolled sneezing. A large white kerchief that had seen better days was employed to collect deposits. It was smeared with dark stains bearing testimony to its repeated visits to the depth of the nasal passage. He would accidentally drop it on the floor while delivering a discourse on the merits of social service from behind the old desk that served as a pulpit for his dispassionate sermons. None would dare to make eye contact with him as he expected one of the boys sitting in the front row to pick up this treasured piece of discolored cloth and respectfully hand it over to him. Finding no takers he would eventually let out a loud sigh of disappointment and pick up the article with the agility of a person twice his age. Undeniably, the science teacher had a talent for capturing the attention of his students and evoking their interest in the subject. For the most part the audience would be spell bound except for occasional distractions when attention would be diverted to a mundane matter. He would attempt to scratch an imaginary itch in his left ear lobe with his right hand going right across the top of his rapidly balding head. As a man of science, he could have set an example in efficiency by utilizing his left hand to realize the same objective. This peculiar habit was in keeping with his teaching style which was to make simple matters appear very complicated. On the other hand the mathematics teacher was equally adept but in the opposite way. A short man with a colourful vocabulary, he went to great lengths to simplify complex principles. These wonderful teachers inspired many in the class to pursue science as a career option. Priests in training constituted a small but influential segment of the teaching faculty. It was customary for these revered teachers to carry a whip that was often used in exercise of the authority they had conferred upon themselves. They would be particularly severe on those students found to be loitering aimlessly while trying to catch the attention of girls on their weekly visit to the nearby church. It was common knowledge that neither the boys nor the girls whom they were pursuing seldom entered the church. These girls were students from a nearby all girls school who had to deal with the discipline imposed by nuns in training serving on the faculty of their own school. Apparently, trainees in long frocks kept an eye out for girls in short skirts. Once trapped, the girls were ordered to undo the stitches on their skirts in order to stretch the fabric to a modest length. Walking home from school, Satyananda would often see a stern nun running in hot pursuit of hawkers who made a living selling street food. Many among the trainees were of European descent and could speak only a few sentences of the local language delivered in a thick accent which the hawkers could scarcely comprehend. The vendors on their part, were not exactly sure as to why they were being chased but were unwilling to challenge authority. Business was good and they wished to keep it that way. Both sides were content with this cat and mouse charade. The sports and drill teacher sported a big paunch and wore undersized clothing. It was rumored that he had political connections and liasing with government authorities on the school's behalf was his real job. His motivational speeches were always a hit, not so much for their content as for their entertainment value. He was a master at creating his own brand of the queen's language employing literal english translations of vernacular sentences. An enterpising boy compiled the most popular sayings of his teacher and made the booklet available to the students for a nominal price.

Text books on history had apparently not been revised since the country gained independance from foreign rule. A historical perspective on India's glorious past would indeed have evoked interest from the students. What was described in the text books on history was essentially a chronicle of foreign rule in India. These boys were born as citizens of a free country after the sun had finally chosen to set over the empire. The jewel had broken free from the suffocating hold of the crown in order to coruscate on its own. Thus it was of little interest to them how the former masters had conquered to stoop and amass a fortune by digging deep into the common wealth. The books described numerous acts and policies passed in pursuit of unsuccesful attempts to subjugate the citizenry of an ancient and advanced civilization that adorned an entire sub continent. For the students, such history was essentially a record of tyranny, deceit and aggression undertaken in pursuance of power and appeasement of unlimited greed. The majority of these so called historical events should have been laid to rest in the graveyard of dust laiden archives. Sadly, they continued to survive in text books, influencing vulnerable minds by seeking to project oppressors as benefactors. Satyananda's interest in the past was limited to memorizing the events and then reproducing them verbatim at the annual examination. Some subjects were tolerated by the majority of students, others were disliked but one in particular was held in contempt. This subject carried what on the surface was a harmless name. One might ask how bad can the subject of craft be? Certainly, this was an appropriate subject matter in the curriculum for students of kindergarten. In what can only be termed as a blatant exhibition of cynical wisdom the powers that be had decided that this seemingly innocuous potion of boredom be administered not in one but three middle years. During these classes students were required to design and produce garments from a variety of fabric, every single one painstakingly handmade with a curse at every stitch. The Gandhi *topi* project was undertaken with unbridled mental aggression quite contrary to the spirit of non-violence promoted by the father of the nation. Sleepless nights were spent in meeting the deadline for completing the nightmarish pyjama project. One failed to understand the merit of having boys master the hem stitch. To her credit, the teacher taught this subject with exemplary dedication and zeal and a passion bordering on fanaticism. As difficult as it is to envision such a scenario, it was not uncommon to see many pupils on their knees in her class, as punishment for not completing the assigned homework. To break the monotony, this teacher was prone to use her knuckles to deliver a sharp tap on the head or a pinch on the upper arm of a kneeling student accompanied by a comical facial contortion. This was apparently meant to add injury to insult. Needless to say, there were many chronic defaulters who preferred such punishment over the drudgery of doing the homework and never reformed despite the best efforts of the said teacher. As with all other subjects, the work was marked. None would wish to top the class, since this would most certainly invite ridicule from less unfortunate classmates.

By and large, students enrolled in this school could be broadly classified into three personality types. First and foremost were students who performed exceptionally well academically but were social outcastes. They congregated in groups to find solutions to complex mathematical problems oblivious to the rest of the class. Students who were apparently quite intelligent but mischevious, by virtue of being under challenged belonged to the second category. Such students were endowed with a talent for art and poetry. Unlike the super intelligent boys in the previous category, they were very liberal in exhibiting their creations for the benefit of all. Examples of their ingenuity were displayed on blackboards, walls in washrooms, fences or even on trees in the school compound. They would faithfully pass the annual examinations each year and be promoted to the next class. The third category consisted of boys who spent multiple years in each successive class, bullying younger class fellows and testing the patience of their teachers. They were apparently content to live their lives one day at a time, free from the anxiety that comes with the setting and achieving of personal goals. Their presence in the classroom was a constant reminder of inadequacies in the system. Expulsion was never an option. In borderline cases, authorities would bend the rules to push them to the next grade until they could not advance any further. It was left to the discretion of their parents to determine if and when they wished to terminate the education of these young adults. Some such scholars were at an age at which no self respecting individual would be seen wearing a school uniform. Their favourite pastime was to make passes at young female teachers in the primary section of the school. Since one had to pass the annual qualifying examination in order to be eligible for promotion, every year there were some in Satyananda's class who had failed to make it to the next grade. Some boys would even warm the benches of the same class for a few years while watching consecutive batches of younger classmates progress to higher grades.

Being the youngest and physically the smallest student in his class Satyananda had no choice but to occupy a seat in the front row. A small lock on the school bag served to protect his meagre treasures from some older boys who were known to borrow articles without the knowledge of their owners. He was constantly bullied by them and their favourite pastime was to tap him on the back of his head. On a fateful day in the fourth grade, he unlocked his bag to quickly withdraw a note book before the teacher walked into the classroom. Absent mindedly he placed the key in his mouth even as a rather obese student delivered a sudden sharp tap on his head. Recovering from the surprise, he realized that he had swallowed the key. On returning home, he related everything that had transpired to his mother. Together they went to consult their family physician. The wise gentleman had a simple remedy to mitigate the risk. It entailed consuming a number of bananas in rapid succession. Apparently, bananas have purgative properties and the bulk provided by consuming several of these, facilitates the object's exit from the other end of the alimentary canal. The process followed in order to ascertain that the key had indeed left the body shall remain undisclosed. Suffice to say that in this particular case, the end clearly justified the means. The treatment led to a satisfactory outcome.

Drill was not a particularly pleasant activity for our hero although he was by and large not averse to physical exertion. For the older boys, the highlight of this activity was the annual parade that terminated at the school for girls. It so happened that in one particular year Satyananda was late for the parade. When he arrived at the school, the marching band was on full blast and the boys were already assembled in neat rows in preparation for the march. On finding the gate locked, he had no option but to jump over the cast iron fence in order to enter the school compound. In the process one leg of his shorts got entangled on the sharp edges of the fence tearing it as he descended on the other side. Fortunately, he was placed in the middle of the bunch. A visibly large split in the garment would have surely received unwanted attention were he to be placed on the sides. His relief was however shortlived as unknown to him a potentially embarrassing situation lay ahead. On reaching the school for girls, the boys were required to perform stretching and bending exercises. Thus a part of his anatomy was exposed to the full view of the female spectators. For many days thereafter, a special joke was circulated at his expense. Misfortunes seemed to follow him home. The occupant of the ground floor apartment of one segment of the building complex exhibited a strong dislike for the pastimes of young children. On one occasion he had chased young Satyananda's friend over several flights of stairs until he finally caught up with the helpless boy. He had then proceeded to give vent to the full force of his mercurial temper by raining blows on the defenseless child. No child would complain to the parents for fear of receiving additional punishment from them. In those days it was common for parents to be under the mistaken notion that their child must have committed an offense in order to be worthy of such treatment from an honourable neighbour. The result would be another round of scolding or a sound thrashing in certain instances. No child was prepared to face a painful repeat of a preceding event. Although there was no dearth of good company during summer vacations, on a particularly lazy day, Satyananda did not find anyone to keep him company. He kept himself busy by repeatedly opening and folding the collapsible cast iron gate at the entrance of one of the wings. By a sheer stroke of luck, Satyananda withdrew his attention momentarily from his preoccupation with the gate long enough to notice this gentleman advancing menacingly towards him. Sensing imminent trouble he did not wait to investigate the reason for the gentleman's displeasure. Taking to his heels he left the building compound at full speed with the said gentleman in hot pursuit. Together they covered a considerable distance on the street passing gaping residents and idle bystanders witnessing the extraordinary spectacle of a young lad outrun a physically fit adult. Every dog has his day but this one belonged to the puppy who was heard repeatedly muttering an apology in a high pitched voice to the bull terrier charging at his rear. At that very moment the powers that be conspired to intervene in favour of the weak and helpless. The situation took a decisive turn. A few stray dogs decided to come to the aid of the underdog. Now the balance tilted in favour of the puppy, as these hitherto idle canines joined the chase. The roles were reversed and now it was the hunter's turn to be the hunted. Under the circumstances it was perfectly justifiable for the villian in the drama to use his reserve strength to meet the immediate demands of self preservation. Throwing caution to the winds, he dodged seemingly unsurmountable obstacles in a frantic attempt to keep man's best friends at bay. After covering a considerable distance in record time he was seen to hastily disappear into a roadside shop. The symphony of woofs, barks and growls continued until these talented artistes were finally driven away by the shopkeeper. Thereupon the perpetually angry young man was seen to emerge from the shop, look sheepishly in both directions before slowly making his way homewards. Satyananda had often fed biscuits to these stray dogs. This small investment had paid rich dividends at the opportune time. From that day onwards this gentleman went to great lengths to avoid eye contact with Satyananda on those few occasions when their paths crossed. With timely and wholehearted support from some friendly quadrupeds, the misfit had shown this tyrant his place.

In matters related to health Satyananda's father was fastidious in the extreme. Periodically, the senior would insist on the son's participation in an internal cleansing ritual. The series was put into motion late on a saturday evening when Satyananda was invited by his mother to partake of a cup of tea. Closer examination revealed an oily substance floating on the top. He was instantly repelled by the beverage when informed that the exhibit was a cocktail of tea and castor oil. Ofcourse resistance would be futile once his father had made up his mind. Numerous visits to the toilet the following day was testimony to the efficacy of the treatment. The taste was horrible and the after effects even worse. Later in life Satyananda had reason to thank his father as he was blessed with excellent health until he was well past his midlife crisis. He would readily admit that thanks to the vitamin pills placed daily on his plate at breakfast, as a youngster he had boundless energy on the playground. Cricket matches with teams from adjoining buildings were frequently organized at a community playground a considerable distance away. Umpires were always from the batting side. The concept of neutral judges was non existent and conflict of interest was never a consideration. The side to bat first would set the criterion for fairplay and players on the opposing team would reciprocate when it was their turn. No quarters were asked and none were given. Players would be declared out only when it was clearly obvious such as when the ball hit the stumps directly or a clean catch was made. Disputes on the umpire's decisions were commonplace and the majority of matches would end in physical fights between domineering players on either side. The outcomes of such matches were predetermined by alpha males on either team whose sole interest in playing the game was to create opportunities for conflict.

Graduation from high school finally liberated Satyananda from the restrictive shackles of the school uniform. He was now free to dress as he pleased although his preference was never aligned with trends in contemporary fashion. Body hugging bell bottom pants were too uncomfortable for his liking. This was his first experience with the co-educational system. While permitting intermingling of genders in the college compound, the system was at the same time ultra conservative when it came to seating arrangements within the classroom. Girls and boys occupied seats on opposite sides of the room. Satyananda went to great lengths to maintain his distance, even prefering to cross over to the other side of the street on seeing a girl approaching him from the opposite direction. He cultivated a strong reading habit and kept himself informed on current affairs. Never a fan of conventional modes of entertainment, he was indifferent to the lure of movies but loved to participate in sporting activities. Describing him as a bookworm would not have been far from the truth. Although he had maintained good scores by burning the midnight oil when necessary, his efforts did not avail against competition from those who could afford to pay for private tuitions. These private coaching classes guaranteed success in qualifying examinations for entry into professional colleges. In the highly competitive Indian education sytem the alternative to a professional degree was to be condemned to a life of perpetual struggle. His parents were unwilling to admit defeat easily even though it appeared to him that the door had been shut on the realization of a fond dream. They encouraged him to enroll in a private engineering college located on a hill overlooking a lush green valley close to the town where he was born. Realizing that paying for his education would put a big dent in their meagre savings, he was initially reluctant to agree but consented only after much persuation from them.

Chasing miseries

It was the beginning of a new era in the life of the misfit. For the very first time this young man had to do his own laundry. After being exposed to the poor quality of food served in the hostel canteen he learned to appreciate the love which his mother put into her cooking. He sincerely regretted having unjustly criticized her for minor lapses in culinary skills. After a few months, his body had adjusted to the poor quality of food to such an extent that it was unable to tolerate the food so lovingly prepared by his dear mother. On returning home to spend his vacations he would suffer from diahorrea as his stomach had apparently forfeited its capacity to retain wholesome and nourishing food. During the first few weeks in the college, he was exposed to the trauma of ragging. This was a time honoured boot camp tradition that enabled seniors to "break in" rookies. The objective was to test their endurance by raising the level of discomfort to a point where many would breakdown and weep. Each new batch of students was subjected to innovative torture techniques that appeared dangerous in theory but were actually harmless in practice. They were designed only to test the capacity of the recipient to withstand persistent assaults on his self esteem. Peculiar physical exercises coupled with the use of abusive language delivered at a high pitch wrecked havoc on the mental state of those individuals who had lived sheltered lives until then. Satyananda kept a very low profile during this time and even contemplated returning home. With great difficulty he managed to survive the daily ordeal of saluting every senior on sight during the day and singing the national anthem to them each evening while being, at the same time, subjected to other modes of humiliation.

By the end of the first semester the former introvert emerged from his self imposed cocoon. He joined the debating and dramatics clubs on campus and even represented the college at inter collegiate elocution competitions. He excelled at sports, chess being his favourite game. Even as he permitted himself to indulge in these extra curricular activities he did not loose sight of his goal of earning his degree in the prescribed timeframe. The same could not be said for some in his class who succumbed to temptations that diverted their attention to activities unrelated to education. These gentlemen were honoured with the title of mighty seniors in recognition of the number of extra years they had walked the hallways as students of this great institution. During their extended internship, the syllabus would have changed with the introduction of a "new scheme" to differentiate it from the "old scheme". Thus a two-tier curriculum was in place to accommodate the late boomers who were required to be tested under the former scheme. The external examiners for practical examinations were drawn from other teaching institutions. They often travelled long distances in order to conduct examinations, sometimes for a single student remaining in the "old scheme" only to find that the examinee had played truant. In his anxiety to end the "old scheme" by clearing its remnants, the principal would send a hastily assembled party to trace and then encourage the reluctant student to attend the practical examination. Students who failed at the first attempt were enrolled in "irregular" batches. Some such students were highly accomplished in designing novel techniques for ragging. One among this species stood out in particular. This mighty senior going by the nickname Sandow was a passionate body builder who had clearly paid undue attention to maintaining a perfect physique at the expense of his intellectual development. He was always eager to demonstrate his superior strength by squeezing the palms of unsuspecting juniors in a manner that would evoke a sharp cry from the unfortunate victims. This was interpreted by the tormentor as an acknowledgement of his prowess. A sinister smirk would appear on his countenance at the end of each such torturous episode. Needless to say, Sandow would avail of every opportunity to repeat the experience. He was also known to take liberties with the articles of daily use belonging to fellow residents of the student hostel. While sauntering to his room after a typical weightlifting session in the gymnasium, he would wipe his profusely perspiring body with towels left out to dry on the common clothesline in the verandah. He would use his own towel only after a prolonged session in the shower. In his myopic vision of the scheme of things, the right to misuse the personal articles of others was conferred on him by virtue of his superior might. Lesser mortals were expected to understand and accept this simple fact of life without contest. Indeed it would be futile to expect resistance from those who lived in fear of even the simple act of shaking hands with the giant. Satyananda was the most frequent victim since his room was adjacent to that of this aspirant for the title of Mr. India. After having silently endured his uncouth behaviour for some time, he devised an evil but brilliant plan to impart a lesson on the importance of civic sensibilities. Satyananda was aware that the local flora supported the growth of a particular species known to be a potent topical irritant much like poison ivy. A scouting trip in the monsoon season yielded a rich harvest of this plant. After having crushed the leaves within the folds of a towel and having masked the odor with a liberal dose of perfume, he hung it at a strategic position on the clothesline. The experiment ran the anticipated course leading to a very satisfactory conclusion. To make a long story short, the guinea pig took the bait and suffered the consequences. The speed of reaction was the sole deviation from the anticipated result. Given the normal lethargic behaviour of this individual, the degree of agility exhibited by Sandow took everyone by surprise. The giant was observed to run helter-skelter like an unrestrained hyperactive child, furiously rubbing his back on every pillar in sight. Finding them rather smooth and unsuitable for the purpose, he graduated to experimenting with trees. In the process he disturbed a few cows who were engaged in the same exercise. Although initially it appeared that the young and restless among them were preparing to meet the challenge, they eventually scattered with the rest of the herd. Their retreat was inconsequential since by then Sandow had finally disappeared into a shower. From there he implored his sidekick to hand over his personal towel to him. At breakfast the next morning, those who dared to approach him, remarked that his face and neck bore telltale marks of a severe allergic reaction. This condition lasted for a number of days until it gradually subsided leaving behind some scars which also vanished eventually. The iron man was reformed to such an extent that he was unwilling to even look in the direction of any article hanging on the clothesline. After having finally completed the five year degree course in nine years, he accepted a position as an inspector of manufacturing units with the provincial civil service. This opened the door to numerous opportunities to recover the money that he had wasted on his college education. He earned a reputation for being particularly strict with companies that were ethical and preferred to play by the rules. His modus operandi was constructed primarily on the premise that his clients had something to hide. Consequently, while the true purpose of the inspection was to unearth fact, he had reduced it to an exercise for finding fault. The inspection would be terminated as soon as a fault was located however inconsequential it might be to the overall quality of the product being manufactured. Companies that were eager to adopt internationally recognized manufacturing practices and standards could never benefit from his inspections since terms such as corrective and preventive actions or remedial measures did not exist in his lexicon. All premises inspected by him could be consistently expected to receive satisfactory ratings without much ado if their owners were willing to engage in appropriate negotiations with him prior to filing his reports. Any resistance offered would be countered with veiled threats of unspecified actions and even closure of the manufacturing unit. As far as he was concerned, when enforcing the law it was imperative that absolute power be exercised however petty the violation might be.

When Satyananda graduated from this college he was prepared to meet the world on his own terms. He had consistently performed well in studies and held numerous certificates that bore testimony to his skills at dramatics, debating and sports. He had big plans for a rewarding career in manufacturing. It did not take very long for the bubble to burst. After several unsuccessful attempts he was able to find a job as a supervisor of the night shift in a manufacturing unit. The company had a history of unrest on account of a militant labour union. The plant manager was stabbed in the back shortly after Satyananda joined the workforce. For several weeks following this incident he kept a hockey stick to defend himself in the event of an unexpected attack from a disgruntled employee. The night shift was notorious for troublemakers. Some would habitually report for duty in an intoxicated state. Strangely enough, these individuals were extremely diligent when they were sober. Through insight gained from experience, Satyananda arrived at the understanding that permitting such employees to rest for a short while at the beginning was reciprocated later in the shift. As a result, among all shifts, the highest productivity was realized during the night. He handled occasional acts of insubordination tactfully, refusing to report anyone to upper management. As per company policy lodging a complaint would automatically lead to disciplinary action against the employee. All concerned were anxious to avoid such possibilities given the adversarial relations between labour and management. The bottom line was that as long as production targets were met, small indiscretions would be tolerated in the larger interest of peace. A few months in this rigorous climate convinced Satyananda that he was not cut out for this task. He found himself placed between two mighty forces with a history of disagreements. This position could prove to be very uncomfortable in the long run. Moreover, he was keen on pursuing advanced degrees. When he was successful in securing admission to a post graduate degree course at a reputed university, he quit with no remorse.

The driver of the autorickshaw had mysteriously lost his way to the university campus in the middle of the night. Satyananda did not know this, as it was his first visit to the city that took pride in being the home town of the father of the nation. The train from Mumbai had been delayed by several hours due to heavy rainfall. With the sound of thunder and lightning in the background, he checked into a hostel room. Students were expected to abide by a strict moral and ethical code if they wished to reside in the hostels. Prohibition was in force in the entire province. Only vegetarian food was served in the dining hall. Communication with locals was initially difficult until Satyananda was able to achieve a reasonable level of proficiency in speaking the provincial language. The majority of students in undergraduate courses were incapable of conversing in the english language as they had completed their schooling in the vernacular medium. Consequently, although english was the official medium of instruction, for all practical purposes the provincial language was the lingua franca. Initially, this was a major handicap in the discharge of his duties as a teaching assistant. Some students took undue advantage of his inability to clearly articulate the questions posed by him during viva voce examinations. He would be requested to translate such questions from english to the vernacular and then provide repeated clarifications on the translations. For their part the teachers were also not fluent in the english language since it was rarely spoken outside the classroom.

Windows in hostel rooms were not barred. Being a chronic somnambulist, this was a safety concern for Satyananda. He could jump out of the window if he did not wake up in time to sense the danger. The result could be a potentially fatal fall to the ground, several floors below. This problem had tormented him since early childhood. On this account, his mother worried about his safety when he was away from home. Various remedies had been tested including a suggestion from a well wisher that beating the sleep walker with a broomstick was the answer to the problem. Apparently, this solution had been tried on other similarly afflicted individuals and had worked like a charm. It seemed that Satyananda was an exception to this rule. When someone had ventured to experiment with Satyananda in the subconscious state, he was severely beaten by him with the same broom. After having turned the tables, Satyananda went back to bed. He had no recollection of the episode the following morning. Those who were aware of his nocturnal tendency were not alarmed on seeing him strolling around aimlessly in the dark with a blank look on his countenance. They would softly coax him to return to bed and he would promptly comply. On one occasion, as a guest at the home of a relative, he had woken up in the middle of the night horrified to find himself in the couple's bedroom. Fortunately for Satyananda, at that moment they were in deep sleep and were therefore blissfully unaware of this intrusion into their privacy. During another episode, he had scared the wits out of his young cousins while performing a song and dance show in his sleep. He had always been careful to forewarn anyone sharing the room with him, to be alert to a possible episode during the night in which case they were to instruct him to return to bed. This was a simple solution that had worked out quite well until that point in time. Unfortunately he had failed to pass on this vital information to his current room-mate. It so happended that on the very first night, Satyananda woke up from deep slumber to find himself standing on the window sill preparing to jump. He realized that divine will had intervened to protect him from serious injury. Looking back into the room he could faintly discern his room-mate cowering in terror concerned for his own well being. Satyananda had to go to great lengths to assure him that he was as harmless when walking in his sleep as he was when awake. Ofcourse this gentleman did not know how to interpret the statement since he had known Satyananda only for a short time. In any case, he had no choice in this matter since all other rooms in the hostel were taken.

The hostel cafeteria only served lunch and dinner. Students had to make their own arrangements for food at other times. Satyananda and his close friends provided steady business to some restaurants on campus that served breakfast very early in the morning. It was understood that every member of his group would settle the common bill when it was his turn to pay. This had worked very well and all were comfortable with this arrangement. However, a particular student not belonging to his regular circle of friends would often partake food at their expense. This individual was also known to take similar liberties with other groups. His modus operandi was to strike a casual conversation with one individual in the group and then gradually slip into a vacant seat at the table. He would then help himself to the food without even so much as offering to pay his share when the bill was presented. Initial attempts to advance the bill in his direction failed since he would skillfully guide it to the next person at the table. This nonchalant attitude infuriated everyone who had suffered his company. Although it was considered discourteous to expect guests to pay, it was essential to make an exception in this case. The situation called for stronger measures of persuasion and even insult if necessary. On a cold winter morning, observing that the group had placed a big order for breakfast, the uninvited guest quickly slid into a seat at the table. Satyananda whispered in his ear that he should place a lavish order since it was the birthday of a member of the group. As expected, the unwelcome guest fell into the trap. Beaming with excitement, he generously added a few items of his own to the already large list. Unbenownst to the guest, the waiter had been taken into confidence and briefed with explicit instructions to present the bill to no other than the parasite. Towards the end of the sumptuous breakfast a member excused himself and left the restaurant. A call was received shortly thereafter. The uninvited guest was informed by the waiter that he was required to proceed to the adjoining room to answer a telephone call. A barely audible voice at the other end informed him that the principal of the college wished to see him in connection with a complaint about an alleged indiscretion on his part. His attempt to seek clarification was cut short abruptly when the caller hung up. Visibly distracted at not having fully understood the conversation, he was in for a shock when he returned to an empty table. Thrusting it towards him, the waiter impatiently demanded that he settle the bill. Refusing to pay at first, he later consented most reluctantly when the owner threatened to report him to the authorities. From that day forward the perennial guest chose to avoid the company of Satyananda and his friends.

When the position of president of the university research student's assocation fell vacant, Satyananda was the natural choice. He was anointed without much fanfare since the association was bankrupt courtesy of his predecessor. Even before he had fully understood the scope of his responsibilities, he was placed in a situation that required him to defend the rights of a research student in the pure sciences faculty with whom he was not acquainted. At that point in time it was considered honourable for research students to allow themselves to be exploited by their preceptors in the hope that their sacrifices would eventually pay rich dividends in the real world. Research students toiled in the laboratories like bonded labourers trying to satisfy their preceptors' thirst for publications. A predetermined number of papers had to be publised in scientific journals by each researcher prior to being released from the unwritten bond. Students were expected to be grateful for the opportunity to learn from the masters. A certain highly acclaimed slave driver had earned a reputation for delaying the graduation of his research students until they met the quota for publications set by him. As a result some students languished in his laboratory for several years. As much as he benefited from the credit received for successes, the professor was quick to ascribe failures to an apparent lack of diligence on the part of the students. Technically, he was supposed to guide them at every step but this was never the case. One student who had suffered this treatment for long decided to rebel against this transparently unfair practice and succeeded in recruiting others to support his cause. The response from the professor was quick and ruthless. The rebel was debarred from the laboratory and asked to vacate his hostel room. To prevent access to personal belongings, his locker was sealed with a big lock on top of his own. A strike called by research students was in progress even as Satyananda was pulled into the conflict. He had not been informed of the impending trouble prior to his acceptance of the position. It dawned on him that he had perhaps been unwittingly sucked into a situation that could potentially affect his chances of graduating early. Satyananda had served in leadership roles in a number of associations during his undergraduate days. His leadership skills had been well appreciated in the past but this was a different kettle of fish. His request for a meeting with the professor was quickly accepted as this experienced manipulator was perhaps intent on teaching the novice a lesson in the art of diplomacy. At the appointed hour, Satyananda made his way towards the professor's cabin accompanied by members of the governing council of the students association. Since Satyananda believed in leading from the front he was the first person to reach the professor's office. On seeing that three faculty members had joined the professor in a show of fraternal unity, he was glad that he had also brought his team members along for support. To his chagrin, not one of them was in sight when he turned around to introduce his team to the professors. Apparently they came, they peeped and they fled before they could be spotted by their professors. Momentarily taken aback, he nevertheless recovered very quickly in time to respectfully acknowledge the presence of the professors in the room. He was asked to take a seat, provide details of his research programme and the identity of his guide. Everything that he blurted out was duly recorded. It was apparent that the professors were preparing to intimidate him into submission. However, they were soon to realize that the individual seated in front of them was a seasoned negotiator. The session commenced with the errant professor accusing students of looking for opportunities to gang up against him. The rebuttal from Satyananda was blunt. He pointed out that in this particular case it was apparently the turn of a student to be outnumbered by four hostile professors. A prolonged dialogue ensued with Satyananda building a strong case in favour of the student, employing demanding and pleading tones alternatively. The professors stubbornly refused to yield to reason, united in the belief that the teacher is always right and the student is expected to fall in line. They made it known that as far as they were concerned unquestioned obedience from students was a prerequisite for fruitful partnerships between researchers and faculty. Gradually the language and tone of the discussion deteriorated with the passage of time as the professors struggled to counter this unexpected challenge to their authority. Since neither party was prepared to yield, a temporary truce was declared around noon and the meeting was adjourned for lunch. During the break, Satyananda took the opportunity to keep his preceptor informed about the developments. He had an excellent rapport with her and had always sought her sage advice on professional as well as personal matters. Reassembling after lunch, the professors were visibly surprised to observe that the student had returned for more despite sustained efforts on their part to make him as uncomfortable as possible. The discussion now took a turn for the better, with the learned gentlemen showing signs of their willingness to compromise. Apparently the dictator had also used the lunch break to complain to Satyananda's preceptor about the rabble rousing tendencies of her graduate student. Whereupon the wise lady apparently took the said professor to task. He was advised to foster conditions that promote mutual respect between the teacher and the taught and not to treat his students as personalized slave labour. Thoroughly chastened by the position taken by his senior colleague, he was open to a mutually agreeable outcome when the meeting resumed. The professors agreed to reinstate the dismissed student on condition that the strike be withdrawn immediately. Both parties found this to be an amicable settlement. Satyananda learned a very important lesson on that day. Indeed, success is assured when one is willing to place the interests of an other individual before one's own. Despite the fact that a large number of research sudents benefitted immensely from his actions, Satyananda did not receive any recognition from his peers. Those who had deserted him at the eleventh hour were anxious to downplay the incident lest their behaviour stand exposed. It dawned on Satyananda that he had perhaps overestimated the capacity of his team to surmount challenges. Seeking recognition from them would be tantamount to honouring these cowards. It would serve no purpose other than to dilute the sense of fulfillment that he felt within.

Graduating with honours, Satyananda was once again set to rejoin the industrial workforce. Before long he came face to face with the harsh realities of discrimintation based on qualifications and level of knowledge. Despite performing well at several job interviews, he was unable to secure a suitable job. He attributed this to insecurity in the minds of academically less qualified individuals occupying senior positions in these organizations. Irrelevant questions were posed to him during interviews. He was even ridiculed when he was unable to provide the precise response that the interviewers had in mind. It seemed the outcome was always predetermined. He was going through the trouble for nothing. After several futile attempts, he finally succeeded in securing a job as a trainee analyst in a reputed company. Though the pittance offered as compensation did little justice to his qualifications, he reasoned that beggars could not be choosers. The alternative was to twiddle his thumb watching time go by unproductively. Although he now had a foot in the door he had to deal with subtle mental torture. The quality control manager who did not see eye to eye with the general manager, entertained a suspicion that Satyananda had been planted by the latter to spy on him. This ill informed attitude was perhaps the result of a sheer coincidence. It so happended that the general manager and the trainee were alumni of the same college. The quality control manager made his suspicion known to a confidant who in turn spread the word to colleagues in the quality control laboratory. They chose to distance themselves from the trainee in order to demonstrate their loyalty to the manager. They were quick to hold him responsible for errors arising from their own incompetence. He was often asked to stay back late to complete work that was not urgent. The quality control manager created opportunities to frequently carry tales to his superior about Satyananda's apparent ineptitude in meeting corporate expectations. The general manager did not pay much heed to these complaints. He had judged Satyananda's potential by posing searching technical questions to him during the interview. Indeed he would have offered him a higher position if one was available. At the end of his probationary period, the quality control manager recommended that Satyananda's service be terminated. At the same time he went to great lengths to extol the abilities of another trainee to whom he was anxious to offer a permanent position. When the two recommendations were placed before the general manager, he proceeded to consult some experienced employees in the quality control department. Their unbiased opinions convinced him that Satyananda was the better choice. The quality control manager did not conceal his bitterness when the decision went in Satyananda's favour. He demanded that the general manager provide him with the rationale for overruling his choice. The former offered to undertake a test that would determine who among the trainees was better suited for the task. Among the many products marketed by the company, the highest selling was a certain mixture of chemicals. A production line was entirely dedicated for its manufacture.

Several batches of this product were produced and tested every month. The general manager devised an ingenious scheme to test the two candidates. On the first three days samples were taken directly from manufactured batches and passed on to the candidates for testing. Results were declared to be comparable. Thereafter, several laboratory scale batches were secretly formulated omitting one or more ingredients from each mixture. When the test results were compared it was clear that in every case only Satyananda had accurately reported the missing ingredients, with due remarks about possible reasons for such omissions. Under interrogation, the other trainee admitted his mistake in every case. He had chosen to manipulate the results rather than repeating the tests to confirm his findings. Although he secured a permanent position, Satyananda was keen to explore possibilities for career advancement elsewhere in the company. Thus when an opportunity in the registration department came his way, he did not hesitate to switch. Although it came with a generous compensation package the position was fraught with challenges. He was required to deal with a government machinery that moved at a snail's pace. Licence was like old wine. It matured in its own time. It had to be coaxed into acceleration through generous financial incentives for its brewer. These were entered as business expenses in the company's accounting system. Time to market was the bottom line. Timely registration of products was key to a quck return on investment. The pressure was intense. Satyananda was often placed in situations that required him to sacrifice values and ethics in the interest of expediency. None of the management courses that he had taken had prepared him for the real world. For sure the importance of ethical behaviour was repeatedly emphasized. Text books on management were written by academicians who seemed to be blind to realities on the ground. Indeed practice was much divorced from theory. He entertained thoughts of resigning during those times when guilt pricked his conscience but he carried on nonetheless. His parents were now actively engaged in seeking a bride for him. In the matrimonial business a prospective groom without a steady source of income would not be a marketable commodity. It appeared wise to live with a moral dilemma rather than to advertise one's inadequacies to the world.

Game set and match

It was Satyananda's turn to experience the intense politics of the barter carried on in the name of sensible match making. Enquiries from parents of eligible brides began to pour in at a rapid pace when his intention to get married was made public. His parents were in ecstacy at the numerous opportunities to recount his professional accomplishments and to exaggerate his sterling qualities. They considered the complements received in return as affirmations of their skill in raising a worthy son. In keeping with the demand, they had put in place an imaginary decision tree that included a stringent process for screening out the unwanted. The groom in waiting was told in no uncertain terms that later on in the process he would be given the opportunity to provide his input. He had to wait patiently until then if he wished to acquire a good life partner. After all, they had his best interests at heart. Who else could be better placed to know his likes and dislikes? Never mind that he had lived away from home for the past few years. Their protocol required that the girl clear a preliminary screening by them at the outset. His protests did not fall on deaf years. They were certainly heard but were interpreted by his doting mother, to be in line with her constantly changing opinion. Conditioned by numerous tongue lashings received over the years from an opinionated partner, his father was anxious to avoid even the suggestion of a potential turmoil. He had absolutely no doubt about his place in the family heirarchy and was more than willing to accept the decisions of his spouse. Potential alliances were shortlisted after the screening process had taken its due course, including detailed enquiries into physical profiles and character traits of the chosen ones. After several rounds of internal and external consultations the list was eventually presented to Satyananda with due remarks. Those consulted were now in the inner circle of trust and were ever eager to prove that they were worthy of the honour. To demonstrate that they had a stake in his future, they worked overtime to feed information to the parents. A few photographs were thrust at him along with a running commentary from his mother on the merits and demerits of each face and the character traits that the pictures did or did not reveal. To please his mother he made a show of carefully examining each one before admitting that he had no idea what he was expected to do with them. Apparently this was exactly the reaction that the mother expected from her son. It was interpreted as a plea from her helpless baby begging her to take charge of the situation. With the air of a mother on a sacred mission, she instructed him to seek the blessings of the presiding deity of a popular temple. He was informed that the desires of some celebrities had been realized after they had fulfilled a vow to walk barefooted from their homes to the portals of this temple. Satyananda had no objection to visiting the temple since he had always revered the gods but he was averse to asking for special favours from them. He felt strongly that destiny should be allowed to take its own course. There should be no attempts to modify by human efforts that which the Lord had chosen to dispense. In any case he felt there was no harm in going through the ritual. When it was duly completed, his mother drew up a weekly schedule to meet prospective brides. After each visit his mother would undertake a laborious exercise in retrospective analyses on the suitability or lack thereof, of each candidate. This included an extrapolation of available information on the beauty, poise, qualifications and home making skills of the subject, the perceived characters of her parents, their financial status and potential share in ancestral property. Satyananda was not taken into confidence in any of these discussions. Another short list was subsequently prepared and presented to him along with a strong recommendation to agree to marry a particular girl. It was no secret that the girl's elder brother was well settled in the USA and her parents had given a verbal undertaking that the brother would sponsor the immigration of his sister and her spouse. Satyananda was repelled by the suggestion that he should barter his life for a chance to live in a foreign country. In any event he was not impressed by any of the girls that he had met to date. No doubt they were all very nice and would certainly make good wives but Satyananda was looking for signs of inner beauty which he was yet to find. None of them had ignited the spark in his heart that would convince him that she was the one. So far he had played the part of an obedient son and a perfect gentleman in the presence of the other parties. It was time to let his mother know that he had neither been amused nor impressed by any girl. To her credit, she took this in her stride unwilling to give up easily. These, she said were the front runners. More photographs of candidates in reserve emerged from the family closet. The process was repeated, with an identical outcome. By then, a disturbing rumour was being circulated. It was impossible to satisfy the demands of this family. Peace prevailed for a short while as his mother became preoccupied with damage control. Then out of the blue a proposal was received through the mail. The letter and the accompanying photograph was handed over to the son without a preamble. The mother had learned from her experience. Taking a quick look at the photograph, Satyananda felt as though he had known this person for a very long time though he was quite certain that he had not met her before. The girl's parents who lived in a different part of the country did not mind travelling to Mumbai. When the two families met, for Satyananda it was love at first sight. Without a single exception, he had carried on conversations with all the girls that he had met previously. This time he did not feel the need to say anything and no one encouraged him to do so. He had made up his mind. He was in a trance throughout the evening. As if in a dream, he could hear his mother putting some questions to the girl.

What is your name?
Kalavati!
Nice name.
Thank you. You are kind!
The name suits you. You are so artistic.
Silence
Do you know that our son is also very talented?
Yes!
You are so slim. You know I was just like you before my marriage.
Silence
Our son likes to eat good food. Can you cook?
A little.

No problem. I was also not a good cook before my marriage but I learned.
Silence

Her soft voice was very soothing to Satyananda's ears. He thought it fitting that unlike in the previous cases when he had travelled to meet the girls, this one had arrived at his doorstep. This was an unexpected but pleasant gift from providence. When the party left, his mother remarked that since he had not spoken a single word throughout the evening, she assumed that he was not impressed. Satyananda replied that his search for a bride had ended. He would marry this girl if she was willing to have him for a husband. Though overjoyed by her son's decision, the mother was not inclinded to communicate the decision immediately to the other party. It was essential that protocol be followed to the letter. However irrational and outdated it might appear to be, the girl's side had to make the first move.

When the bride's parents finally called, Satyananda's mother offered to host them so they could negotiate the next course of action. Now it was Satyananda's turn to lay down some conditions. He insisted that the marriage ceremony be simple. His mother pleaded with him that she be given an opportunity to meet the expectations of their relatives and friends. Being philosophically divorced from a society that believed in pomp and show, he was unwilling to agree to anything that would be a burden on the bride's family. In order to ascertain that his wishes were communicated accurately, he demanded that he be allowed to participate in the negotiations. When his future in-laws learned about his preferences they were quick to point out that their daughter had expressed similar sentiments. There was something happening at a deeper level. Could a brief fortuitous encounter lead to a meeting of minds? Yet it was clear that destiny had conspired to bring together two individuals who had met but once during which none had spoken directly to the other. Alliances are perhaps made in heaven and then cemented on earth aided by a mysterious invisible force powered by the beating of two hearts in unison. Satyananda had read somewhere that the beauty of such marriages is in the opportunities it presents for witnessing the gradual unfolding of the partner's qualities. He had also heard it said that the word wife was actually an accronym for **W**orries **I**nvited **F**or **E**ver. By treating the happiness of the spouse as the ultimate reward for all his endeavours a wise person could perhaps tranform the same into **W**isdom **I**nvited **F**or **E**ver. So it transpired that two families came together on a fateful day to celebrate the union of two strangers embarking on a journey to discover each other.

When life returned to normal, Satyananda realized that he could no longer take liberties with his time. His better half would be waiting patiently for his return. Together they would go out for an evening stroll through the park. It seemed that everyone had special sympathy for the newly married bride. His colleagues would point to the clock at the appointed hour. His parents found excuses to visit their relatives and his close friends chose to keep their distance. Though his life had been mortgaged to another he felt no remorse at his loss. It was true that living for others made life worthwhile. Satyananda felt truly fulfilled when their daughter arrived. He had to surrender another part of his bedroom and the bundle of joy made sure he was kept awake at night. All his time was spent between work and home. He was constantly reminded that it was time to begin saving for the child's future. A father is expected to take comfort in the popular sentiment that somewhere down the road he will receive a return on his investment. God willing one day he will have the opportunity to give away his daughter in marriage. *Kanyadaan* occupies the highest level in the pyramid of charitable donations. It is believed that the bride's parents will earn incalculable merit on undertaking this noble and selfless act. Indeed it is truly a blessing to beget daughters since their arrival tends to civilize the father. Satyananda began paying close attention to the manner in which he was earning his living. Maintaining status quo was no longer an option. The urge to earn his daily bread in a righteous manner overpowered the temptation to maintain a comfortable lifestyle by whatever means, fair or foul. The dishonourable act of passing envelopes in return for a promise to push the file forward was gradually becoming an unbearable burden. Unfortunately, the ability to meet project timelines was the sole yardstick by which the level of his competence was judged. Satyananda no longer believed in meeting the performance targets set for him if it meant being a party to corruption. Although inwardly content, unmet expectations provoked frequent verbal lashings from superiors. Giving due consideration for his track record, he was given a short reprieve with a warning that this would be his final opportunity to redeem his previous status as a star performer. This acted as a nucleus for deep introspection on the importance of ethics and human values. For long, he had chosen to sell his soul as a necessary compromise for accommodating the needs of the body. He experienced a deep sense of liberation when he finally handed in his letter of resignation. After the euphoria died down he began to doubt whether he had made the right decision. Had he acted in haste? Several months passed without a job offer. In desperation he started a small consulting company. The income was meagre but at least it kept his mind occupied. His misery was partially relieved when he was informed that his application for immigration had been accepted by the Canadian High Commission. Beginning life afresh in a new country would undoubtedly be challenging but anything would be an improvement over his current lot. He loved his country dearly but it seemed to him as though the motherland could not provide him sustenance and was wishing that he leave to seek more hospitable pastures elsewhere in the world. The move to Canada brought in its wake a considerable change in Satyananda's personality. Providing for his family would henceforth be the only priority for him. He had been very athletic during his student days. He had neither the time nor the inclination to participate in sporting activities in his adopted country. This was a man on a mission to surmount all obstacles. Success would undoubtedly come with a price tag but turning back to the life he had left behind was not an option. He was living in Canada yet he never permitted his heart to leave India. Providence had apparently decided to refit his personality to suit the new environment while ensuring that the core remained unchanged. Home is indeed where the heart is!

Flight of fancy

The Air India flight was delayed by a dozen hours. The jumbo jet landed at JFK airport well past midnight. Tired and miserable, Satyananda sat down on a bench in a largely vacant airport wishing he had never left the comfort of home. The electronic display indicated that the last flight scheduled for that night had just landed. A cab driver with oriental features who had evidently come looking for passengers arriving on this Korean Airlines flight offered to drive Satyananda to a hotel in downtown New York. On learning that he had to catch a flight to Toronto from La Guardia airport later in the morning, the cabbie offered to take him there. Satyananda declined the offer since he had been forewarned about the risk of engaging taxis after dark in New York. Since there were no arriving passengers left in the airport, the driver was willing to accept even a token amount in lieu of driving a vacant taxi back to the city. Satyananda could not refuse. He thought he would be safe if he sat directly behind the driver's seat. He loosened the buckle on his trousers just in case he had to use his belt as a weapon in self defence. On arriving at La Guardia airport, he wished he had stayed back at JFK. This airport was completely deserted save for some giant humans singing and dancing in a corner of the departure lounge. Satyananda found a couch and slid down into the seat to stay out of sight of the merry makers. After what might have been the longest night of his life, the sun rose and he felt safe enough to venture to the bathroom dragging two large suitcases behind him. Despite the ruckus raised by the group in the background, it had been a lonely night for him.

The immigration officer at Toronto's Lester Pearson Airport spoke slowly and deliberately while looking directly into his eyes. He was making sure that Satyananda understood every word. Satyananda felt very uncomfortable. Back home it was considered impolite to look directly into another's eyes. One stared at the other only when challenged. Even his pet dog would avert its gaze if he looked directly into the eyes while holding its head between his palms. If this was acceptable behaviour in North America, then he would have to get used to it very quickly. The officer asked a few questions.

> *Bonjour! English or French?*
> *Indian*
> *I mean, would you prefer to speak in English or in French?*
> *English*
> *Welcome to Canada*
> *Thank you*
> *I see that you have a good education. We need more people like you.*
> *Thank you sir!*
> *How soon do you expect to find a job?*
> *Don't know. This is my first time.*
> *You speak good English. You will do fine.*
> *Thanks for the encouragement.*
> *I see that you have a family.*
> *Yes, my wife Kalavati and our year old daughter Swasti.*
> *Why did they not accompany you on this trip?*
> *I need to find a job and a decent place to live. Then I will definitely summon them.*
> *Are you sure?*
> *Yes sir, absolutely sure!*
> *You are a wise man.*
> *Thank you sir!*
> *Take care. Remember, in Canada we drive on the right side of the road.*

The officer seemed to be confused by his body language when Satyananda responded by nodding his head. Perhaps that which was considered an affirmative nod was interpreted as the opposite in this part of the globe. He will have to work on understanding the accent and the body language. Formalities completed, Satyananda stepped out into the reception area and was warmly greeted by a relative who had come to receive him. The biting cold was a quick reminder that the winter had set in. The ground was covered with a blanket of snow. He wished he was somewhere else but now was not the time to indulge in self pity. It was necessary to stay focused. He heard someone complaining that the government should be paying its citizens just for living in this inhospitable climate. Satyananda felt that the sentiment of this gentleman was misplaced. Was he unaware that the United Nations had declared Canada as the best country in the world? Less fortunate people would give anything for a chance to live here. It took only a short walk to the parking lot for Satyananda to revisit his opinion. Even the rats did not seem to venture out in this climate. Perhaps there was some merit to the gentleman's outburst after all.

Days went by rapidly while Satyananda actively pursued job opportunities. He was willing to accept the first offer that came along. After several unsuccessful attempts he finally managed to secure a job in a store with minimum wages as compensation. He reasoned that his meagre earnings would at least pay for the rent of the tiny basement apartment to which he returned at the end of a tiring day. It was time to summon his wife and baby daughter. With the reunification of the family came the realization that sooner or later they would have to adjust to the new culture. The fundamental question was whether it would be wise to adopt it entirely or merely adapt to it. It appeared pointless to argue with individuals who held the opinion that adopting the new culture should be made mandatory for immigrants. He was very clear in his own mind that he had moved to the west in order to experience the work culture that he admired so much and not the social culture. He was not inclined to surrender his mother culture since he appreciated its true value. He was not particularly in favour of succumbing to societal pressures in order to gain acceptance. In his estimate, this was a satisfactory compromise that permitted him to enjoy the best of both cultures. He was amused to learn that integration into North American society could be simplified when given names were abbreviated. In many cases the adopted names were unrelated to the original versions. Human ingenuity can be at its very best when faced with unlimited opportunity for creativity. Personal nomenclature could be subjected to innovative redesign in order to be North American compatible. Thus Hari and Vijaya were transformed to Harry and Virginia! He was confronted by a dilemma at his very first workplace. Evidently, his name was a novelty to the manager. Satyananda could sense that he was having difficulty recalling his name and on a few occasions had indirectly suggested that he adopt a North American name. To Satyananda's untutored mind, adoption would be relevant only in the context of an orphan status. He did have a given name and a distinct identity associated with it. Creating an entirely new one would entail the destruction of an existing identity. This was unacceptable to him. Although blending-in appeared to be the least painful option, his conscience did not permit him to accept it. Despite repeated promptings from his superior, he chose not to respond until that memorable day when the manager addressed him in the unpardonable term "hey you". This was the proverbial straw that broke the camel's back. Until then Satyananda had permitted his survival instincts to overrule the dictates of his ego. After all, having to support a family on unfamiliar territory was a perfectly legitimate excuse for swallowing his pride. Also, the fact that this gentleman was physically twice his size was an obvious deterrent that prevented him from doing anything that he would regret later. Yet, this individual's choice of words had triggered a sensitive nerve in Satyananda's cerebral wiring compelling him to protest this blatant exhibition of insensitivity. Had he travelled ten thousand miles to have his identity obliterated in such a fashion? The situation called for a novel approach. The need of the hour was to ensure that big bird's feathers were not unnecessarily ruffled by his solution to the problem. Humpty Dumpty had to be pushed off the wall in a manner that would not shatter his ego to pieces. Necessity, they say, is the mother of invention. Satyananda calmly approached his superior with a note carrying his name in bold upper case. He instructed his manager to retain the note in his pocket and to consult it before calling out to him again. He proceeded to educate this gentleman on the meaning of his name and the importance of pronouncing it in the correct manner. The fact that a name could have deep spiritual significance was a revelation to the manager. Happily for Satyananda, his superior had perfected his name by the end of that day.

Although the job offered relative security, the family could barely make ends meet on his meagre salary. It did not do justice to his qualifications or experience. He was treated on par with members of staff who were mainly dropouts from high school. Helpless when electronic calculators did not function during power outages, they would rely on Satyananda to derive the total amount owed for purchases manually while customers waited impatiently. This was by no means an intellectually stimulating environment. Satyananda felt increasingly frustrated with each passing month. All he had to show for his efforts at finding suitable employment in his chosen field was a rapidly growing pile of rejection letters. Apparently he was either under or over qualified for most jobs. Every letter received ended with a standard promise from the signatory that his application would be placed in the "active file". At first he felt encouraged that he was at least receiving a positive response from the companies. Their silence over prolonged periods confirmed his suspicion that the term "active file" was in fact an oblique reference to the garbage bin. Everyone was apparently looking to hire a person with Canadian experience. How could he gain such experience without being offered a job in the first place? In a moment of weakness, he wrote a strongly worded letter to the provincial minister for industries complaining bitterly about the indifference shown to his qualifications and industrial experience. A quick response from the minister's office offered a ray of hope. An appointment was set up with the minister's personal assistant. This lady was initially very courteous while giving him a patient hearing. After Satyananda had been given a reasonable opportunity to state his case, there followed a long lecture on ways and means to improve his resume. Once again a dead end! It had been a complete waste of time which he could scarcely afford since he worked on daily wages. Thoroughly dejected and demoralized from this experience, he considered returning to India. He was acutely conscious that his market value was diminishing with each passing day. It was necessary to make a decision whether to stay and fight the situation or to succumb and take the flight home. By a stroke of luck an advertisement for an opening in the federal civil service caught his eye while glancing through the local newspaper that had been discarded on a seat in the metro train. The requirements for the position matched his education and skills. This newly found hope encouraged him to delay his plans to return home. He was eventually successful in the written examination and having done very well in the interview, was offered the job. He felt a deep sense of gratitude to the Indian education system which had prepared and enabled him to top the civil service examination in a foreign country.

Such is life

Newcomers are soft targets for unsolicited advice. In the early days, maintaining a single language at home and elsewhere was the buzz concept. At that time, many in the expatriate community were of the opinion that the mother tongue was an unnecessary burden on the children. It was their belief that since the children would be building their future in the country in which they were being raised it would be in their best interest to adopt the local language and customs. Satyananda had great respect for the richness of the English language. It was useful to him in his quest for earning a decent living. However, there is such a thing as love for one's mother tongue. English can only be the step mother language for those who have inherited a genuine mother tongue. Indeed, he felt that forgetting the mother tongue was akin to disowning one's mother which in his estimate was an unpardonable sin. In his opinion, culture could not be divorced from language otherwise there would be no such thing as the Italian, French or German cultures. It would be incorrect to assume that Indian culture could be transmitted entirely in the English language. For his family, persistence had paid rich dividends as their children were fluent in their mother tongue as well as in English. They could converse easily with their grandparents living in India who spoke little English. Consequently, they were always eager to visit relatives in India with whom they had a wonderful relationship. There were many in their friend circle whose children refused to visit India because they could not adjust with relatives primarily on account of the language barrier. The parents took turns to travel to India so that at least one parent could take care of their children in Canada while the other was away.

The question of language became critical when their first born was ready to make an entry into the Canadian education system. Kalavati and

Satyananda had been raised by conservative parents with unshakable faith in tradition and culture. No language other than the mother tongue was permitted to be spoken at home. Their daughter Swasti could converse fluently in her mother tongue and she also spoke English, albeit with an Indian accent. After a few months in elementary school, the student advisor requested a meeting with the parents during which she attempted to make a case for using only the English language at home. In essence, she was recommending that the child should be discouraged from speaking the mother tongue. Satyananda and Kalavati tried their best to explain that languages come easily to Indians and should not pose a problem to their daughter once she was able to make a few friends at school. The advisor was unwilling to bend, going so far as to suggest that by resisting the change, the parents were not working in the best interest of their child. Satyananda was willing to concede that since Canada received immigrants from many countries where English was not spoken, the advisor could not be faulted for taking a rigid stance in this matter. However, some flexibility was in order in a case where both parents were fluent in the English language and were perfectly competent to tutor their child in the medium of instruction. The advisor was showing visible signs of impatience as the discussion progressed. Apparently she was unaccustomed to parents challenging her advice, particularly those who had not lived too long in the country. It was clear that the honourable lady had not previously encountered such a level of assertiveness from recent immigrants. She was determined to convince the parents that they were resisting a simple and sensible solution to what she believed to be a major issue. On the other hand Satyananda did not have an iota of doubt in his mind that this was a nonissue. Yet he was eager to break the stalemate and arrive at an amicable resolution. From the very beginning of the meeting her strong accent and mispronunciation of certain words had convinced Satyananda that English was not the native language of the advisor. While complementing her on her fluency in the language he made it known that it was obvious to him that English was not her mother tongue. The advisor took the bait thanking him for the complement while admitting that French was her first language. Maintaining a facade of feigned innocence, Satyananda enquired whether English was the preferred language at her own home. With unconcealed pride she boasted that her children were fluently bilingual thanks to her insistence on the use of French at home. Suddenly there was panic in her voice as it dawned on her that she was preaching that which she did not care to practice. Further verbal communication was rendered unnecessary. The message was duly received and understood. It was time for Kalavati and Satyananda to quietly rest their case. Clearly, the entry of logic into the deliberations had coincided with the exit of her confidence. In a barely audible voice she indicated that the parents were free to exercise their discretion in the matter of using the English language at home.

Keerti, their second daughter arrived on a cold winter night. The gestation period had been difficult due to a rare complication that could have potentially led to a miscarriage. Complete bed rest was advised for the mother and she had complied unconditionally. A nasty snow storm was raging as Satyananda drove Kalavati to the hospital. Her gynaecologist arrived a little later. Having been awakened from deep sleep by the nursing staff he looked disheveled and quite grumpy. After a cursory examination of his patient he announced that the baby was not due for at least another six hours. He would return in the morning. The couple was left on their own in the preparatory room while the nurse went about her business. Within the hour, in a soft voice Kalavati informed Satyananda that the baby was on its way and he should summon the nurse immediately. In response to the urgent demand of the call button, the nurse made a hurried appearance demanding a reason for the urgency while reminding everyone of the doctor's proclamation that the baby was not due for the next several hours. Nonetheless she reluctantly proceeded to examine the patient. Thereupon her face reflected a series of emotions in rapid succession beginning with disbelief, followed by horror and ending in panic. It was clear from her reaction, that the situation had taken a serious turn. She rushed out of the room and returned shortly thereafter with two residents and a cleaning lady. When things were under control and the baby had been delivered by the resident, in a very soft tone the nurse sheepishly remarked that the mother had been unusually quiet throughout the ordeal. Satyananda had new respect for the patience, courage and will power of his wife. In the midst of furious activity, she had the presence of mind to instruct him to check the time of birth. This vital information would later be conveyed to her parents in India for the preparation of the child's horoscope. No matter is trivial to the mother when it comes to protecting the interests of her child. In Kalavati's estimate it would be unpardonable to allow a lapse in tradition even in the middle of a crisis unfolding in a foreign land.

Among the first lessons Kalavati and Satyananda had learned on their arrival in the dominion was that in North America babies were subject to a colour code. Little boys are dressed in blue, little girls in pink and never the twain shall meet! Due to this colour barrier, they were compelled to refuse blue dresses presented to their daughters by their relatives back home. Their apologetic explanations were a source of much amusement for their country cousins. It was common knowledge that *desi* veterans in North America had pioneered a new tradition requiring babies to bear two names at birth. The first and middle names were derived from the North American and Indian cultures respectively. It could also be the other way around. One name was given exclusively for use by family and friends. The other was meant for the convenience of strangers who could later become friends or even family. Kalavati and Satyananda refused to endow their children with dual identities. Numerous attempts were made by all and sundry to give a native twist to the children's names. All attempts failed miserably in the face of exemplary fortitude from their children. They refused to answer to any names other than those given to them at birth. They also made extraordinary efforts to educate their friends on the correct pronunciation.

Time passed by rapidly as the couple was engrossed in raising two children even as they placed their own lives on hold. Evenings would be typically devoted to tutoring the children. Weekends were mainly reserved for driving the children to different locations in the city. The parents felt it was necessary to provide opportunities for their children to acquire skills in various sports, learn classical music, Indian language and heritage. While they did have friends at regular school, it was very important for them to interact with peers raised in their native culture. Thus although weekends should have been devoted to getting some well deserved rest, this was rarely the case. The parents were often more exhausted on weekends than they were during the week. Every experience is novel to the new immigrant who is, at least in the initial years, on a cultural and materialistic pilgrimage. The progress of the pilgrim depends on a willingness to adapt rapidly to each situation. The normal flow of immigrant traffic is from countries that are developing to those that are considered to be developed. Accustomed to living austere lives, the new immigrants see waste in the midst of opulence. This sentiment may not necessarily be shared by the natives. Immigrants are on a mission to better their own lives and to help improve those of their relatives back home. Every shopping trip is an adventure. At every store the newcomer is constantly alert to the possibility of items available on clearance. When spotted, the items on the rack will be rummaged with the same zeal as a child looking for hidden eggs at an Easter bunny hunt. This is a year round activity since a trip back home is complete only when a gift for every relative is accounted for in the luggage stuffed to the limit of the weight permitted by the airline. Gradually bargain hunting becomes a way of life and the experience gained is eventually passed on to the next generation as a tradition. Everyone in the bargain hunting network is alerted to latest developments. Details of merchandise are communicated either verbally or electronically. Information is extensive when its dissemination is verbal. Typing is a waste of time and it may be too late if recipients do not access e-mails on time. This is also a favourite topic at social gatherings, rendering segregation of genders a practical proposition and not merely a cultural ideal. It is important to keep track of deals missed while the family is away on vacation. Friends save flyers for each other. You see, there is a pattern to discounted prices. Those in the know can actually predict which items are likely to be put on sale at any given time during the year. Apart from the routine ones there are also seasonal sales. No one in their right minds would purchase winter clothes in winter. They are purchased towards the end of winter when they are available on sale at less than half the original price. Sale is a strange game. Often a larger pack that is on sale will be priced lower than a smaller size that is not on sale. The two sizes are placed side by side on the shelf defiantly challenging the consumer to make the logical choice.

Satyananda had always believed that one should have the courage to stand up for one's convictions. New immigrants are under constant pressure to conform to local practices often against their better judgement. In the early days, maintaining a green lawn was a favourite pastime. This was encouraged by aggressive advertising from promoters of fertilizers and pesticides. Satyananda was convinced that this practice was a potential environmental disaster. He had read many research articles describing the toxic effects of pesticides on the reproductive capacities of marine species.

He had also witnessed strong allergic reactions in children who had come in contact with lawns treated with pesticides. Therefore he stubbornly refused to fall in line. As a result, their front lawn was home to a variety of weeds. At first he received subtle warnings through disapproving looks from neighbours. When nothing was done, garbage and on occasion, empty beer cans and bottles were scattered on their lawn. By then Kalavati was showing signs of nervousness but Satyananda was mentally prepared to face such hostility. One day while she was planting seasonal flowers in their garden a middle aged couple stopped by to admonish Kalavati on the state of their front lawn. Satyananda was clearing debris behind a large tree and was hidden from view. On hearing strange agitated voices he emerged from behind the tree and was greeted by a volley of strong words.

Your lawn is a disgrace!
What are your expectations?
For starters you can have the lawn sprayed to remove the weeds.
I am sorry but I refuse to use pesticides on my lawn.
Everyone does it so what is your problem?
Pesticides are not good for the environment. They pollute the water table.
That's bull shit!
It is causing allergic reactions in my children.
Well I am sure your physician can help you deal with that.

The visibly distraught couple threatened to file a complaint with the municipal authorities. Satyananda realized these were empty threats when no action materialized throughout that summer. He put up a sign to the effect that his lawn was pesticide free and therefore safe for use by children. Mothers with young children came forward to congratulate the couple for their courage. They even took pictures of their children posing beside the sign. Subsequent developments vindicated Satyananda's bold stand. Over the next few years, a few well informed neighbours followed his lead to make their properties pesticide free. Following determined lobbying by environmental activists, a decade later municipal authorities voted to discontinue the practice of spraying pesticides on municipal property.

Satyananda had discovered that social drinking had been perfected to a fine art by his compatriots. It enjoyed a very respectable status in North American society unlike in India where consuming alcohol was frowned upon. With the aid of useful tips from those who shared his interest in spirits, he was able to maintain popular brands of liquor in his domestic inventory. From preliminary experiments he had concluded that alcohol helps to cloud the intellect and loosen the tongue. This was indeed a wonderful way to unwind, pontificate or otherwise exhibit one's intelligence to a captive audience of inebriated individuals. While ice breaking conversations were by and large congenial, their quality would gradually plunge as the spirits took control. After exhausting vocabularies on criticising their employers, politicians and the prevalent social system, participants would then divert their attention to finding solutions for the numerous problems in India. At the very least, they felt a moral obligation to comment on the gigantic issues confronting their relatives back home. Predictably, the discussions would focus on negative aspects such as corruption and hygiene, or lack thereof. Positive aspects were rarely under scrutiny since they were perceived to be mundane or otherwise provided little entertainment value. Satyananda soon realised that exposure to such negativity would adversely influence his children's sentiments for that great country. Children raised in such environments could not be faulted for showing disrespect to their ancestral land. He was faced with a conundrum. Despite being aware of the consequences of his action, until that point in time, he had felt obligated to serve alcohol as a token of courtesy to invited guests. With Wholehearted encouragement from Kalavati, Satyananda decided to banish liquor from their home. With this, their social circle vanished mysteriously and so did their anxiety about children being exposed to undesirable influences. Abstinence from spirits opened the door to spiritual gatherings. Graduating from the narrow confines of domestic socializing, the family discovered the world of spiritual congregations. It was as though this treasure had all along been waiting to be mined while Satyananda had been preoccupied with mortgaging his conscience to pay for trivial sensual pleasures. For long he had chosen to speak the language of ignorant sceptics, letting down his ancestors in the process. There followed a period of introspection, self denigration, guilt and remorse at having not only voluntarily surrendered a noble culture received by him as inheritance but also leaving behind a corrupted version of the same for his children. Surely, he was no different from birds and animals whose sole purpose in life is to eat, procreate and eventually perish. Common sense had finally prevailed. He saw no other option before him than to retrace his path and return to his roots. It became imperative to sustain scriptural sanctity within the precincts of his house. His wife and he opened their home and hearts to saffron. Sages who are treasure houses of eternal wisdom counsel that spirituality promotes beauty of the body, maturity of the mind and illumination of the intellect. Possessing the ability to separate the real from the virtual and the truth from illusion, these selfless human beings should rightfully inherit the role of guides for humanity. Self discovery is too frightening to contemplate for many humans, given the abundance of dirt accumulated within. Fortunately, providence had bestowed on Satyananda, the wisdom to seek refuge in the secure womb of his heritage. Yoga, chanting, prayers and meditation became part of his daily routine. Leaving his origins and the land of the Gods behind, he had travelled half way across the globe only to realize that the ancestral culture that he had inherited was his ultimate refuge.

The momentum was building up towards Y2K. Several months before the dawn of the fateful day that would herald the turn of the century, consultants were actively engaged in educating the public on the inevitability of a systemic crash in the electronic environment. The media was also on the bandwagon competing to provide maximum exposure to these dooms day gurus. The problem was attributed to a computer programme that had become obsolete in the western world. The year came and went and everyone breathed a sigh of relief when the anticipated chaos never materialised. It was a good year for the body shops that were busy unleashing hastily trained recruits from India to operate the software programmes that had long been discarded in the west. Many such recruits came to North America on short term visas and never left. Concurrently the high tech boom was at full blast with companies, small and large, competing to attract a limited pool of talent. Manpower was literally recruited from the streets. All those who applied for technician positions were given an opportunity to try their skills. Those who had never worked in blue collar jobs but were unwilling to miss the opportunity to be gainfully employed soon realised they were not cut out for this kind of work. Many were well past their prime and a few came out of retirement. Those hired in haste were eventually fired at leisure when they were found to be unfit for the assigned tasks. In one particular case, those declared surplus received an e-mail asking them to assemble in the cafeteria. Once there, they were served with pink slips and escorted to the gate by security staff. They were not allowed to return to their units as they could potentially wreak vengeance on their employer by corrupting the electronic network. Needless to say, both the human resources and the manufacturing departments were working long hours, the former to welcome and the latter to let go. At the white collar level, many were enticed by the lure of the almighty dollar to leave secure civil service jobs in pursuit of lucrative positions in the private sector. The optimists referred to it as sharing of intellectual property for the common good. The pessimists used the term "intellectual prostitution" to express their contempt for the same phenomenon. No one was immune to its influence. Many chose to move with the flow. To them this was a great opportunity to milk a cash cow. Individuals who were otherwise well balanced succumbed to the fever of job hopping tempted by attractive stock options. When the bubble burst start-up companies began to collapse like a deck of cards. All of a sudden the stocks from these companies were worth no more than the paper on which they were printed. The dreamers were now waking up to the realization that their wealth had been nothing but *maya,* a passing illusion. Those who had been engaged in endlessly recounting the killing they had made in trading day stocks were now silent, too embarrassed to admit that they had nothing to show for their hard work. Like minded people who had come together to form investment clubs in order to benefit from collective wisdom were left with nothing other than memories of the short lived excitement. Many tried desperately to regain the very positions in the civil service that they had contemptuously discarded a few years earlier. Satyananda was unaffected by all that was taking place around him. He had never considered forfeiting his position in the civil service. He had previously experienced the sense of desperation that comes from being unemployed. Thus he was unwilling to gamble with security. While his friends were preoccupied with accumulating imaginary wealth, he had quietly moved up the promotional ladder to reach the top. He had won recognition from his peers and superiors for his deep knowledge of the subject matter. When jobs became scarce in the private sector, those who had previously left in a hurry were now eager to compete for any available positions including those which were well below their level of expertise. It was again respectable to work for the government. Patience had indeed proved to be rewarding for Satyananda, though it had been severely tested at times.

Tribulations in progress

Fear of the unknown haunted these immigrants at every step as Swasti entered high school. Their first born was a dependable teacher since the parents also learned from the experience gained by the child. They had often heard horror stories about the bullies, the alcohol, the drugs and weapons on high school premises. Every so often, Swasti would announce that the police had returned with their dogs to her school and some kids had been arrested for pushing drugs. Each request from their child for participation in school gatherings and private parties was approached with anxiety and suspicion. Consent was subject to the child providing minute details such as the location, the duration of the event and a list of fellow participants. The child was expected to put forward repeated requests for the same event and each episode was tantamount to an interrogation. Approval was delayed as much as possible and when given, came with conditions that severely restricted the movement of the child. It was made to appear that consent was being granted under duress. It came with the explicit understanding that participation in future events would be in jeopardy should the child dare to cross established boundaries. The long list of rules was expanded with each event. The party to celebrate graduation from high school was feared the most. Despite receiving intense coaching from Kalavati, Swasti succumbed to pressure from her peers. In keeping with the current fashion she was inclined to opt for an evening gown. Kalavati was unhappy with this decision.

> *Return the gown. It is not covering enough of your body. The neckline is too deep! The price is also outside my budget for this event.*

Your budget is not enough to buy a decent dress. My friends will laugh at me.
I have pressures of my own. Betty's mother is very pushy. She wants to make sure that your dress is coordinated with Betty's.
So? Do you have a problem with that?
Yes. She has already purchased Betty's dress. I was not consulted. Now she is trying to make sure that I buy a similar gown for you. This is not fair!
Life is not always fair Ma! You told me that yourself!
She is also expecting both of you to wear matching stockings and shoes. I don't like my girls wearing fancy items. I will not permit you to wear heels!
Ma! Everyone will be wearing heels.
They are not good for your back. My colleague at work is always complaining of backache. She knows it is from elevator heels but she is short and wants to look tall.

The debate continued for several days until there was little left to be said. In any case, by then the mother and daughter were barely on speaking terms. It was essential to break the stalemate and resume negotiations. Both turned to the only male member of the family to play the role of an unbiased mediator. Satyananda had silently witnessed the prolonged tussle after being warned to keep his mouth shut when he had offered to mediate early in the contest. Although covertly he sympathized with his daughter, he was nonetheless reluctant to displease his better half. Experience had taught him that marital life is a bed of roses only when the spouse does not prefer thorns. Progress was made when Swasti reluctantly agreed to her mother's suggestion to cover the deep cut in the dress with an embroidered fabric. It was agreed that high heels could be worn only when getting down from the limousine and making a grand entry in the hall. Flat designer shoes would adorn the feet at all other times during the evening. Having successfully mediated a satisfactory resolution, Satyananda permitted himself the luxury of letting out a sigh of relief. It turned out to be premature. A new factor emerged on the day of the event. Kalavati was concerned that her daughter may have applied excessive make up while Swasti argued that it was barely enough. Intervening again Satyananda made an attempt to negotiate another compromise. Once again this was vigorously contested by both parties. A truce was eventually declared leaving the father as the sole satisfied participant. His relief was short-lived since it transpired later that the wife was waiting for the daughter to depart so that she could give him a piece of her overtaxed mind. She was livid that he had broken the golden rule of domestic harmony by supporting the daughter against her at a very crucial juncture in the negotiations.

> *Your daughters will never learn to respect my opinion if you keep on contradicting me.*
> *You were interrupting while I was speaking.*
> *So what is wrong with that? You do it all the time!*
> *This is not about me, it is about Swasti.*
> *I have no freedom in this house! I am not even allowed to interrupt my husband. You have always treated me differently.*
> *I have been married only once. I have no previous experience.*
> *At least you can learn from other husbands. Ashutosh is so thoughtful. He is always buying gifts for Annapoorna.*
> *Maybe he has something to hide.*
> *Why do you always think that others are wrong and you are right?*
> *This is not about you and me, it is about Swasti!*
> *Don't try to change the topic!*
> *What is the topic?*
> *You have never allowed me to do what I want!*
> *Is that the topic Kala?*

By then Satyananda was upset enough to throw caution to the winds. In the heat of the moment, he had failed to put recently acquired theory into practice. By his reaction he had demonstrated that the anger management course completed by him as part of his professional development was of little value in real life situations. Strong words were exchanged and events from the distant past were unhesitatingly dragged into the present in order to strengthen the respective positions of the disputing parties. There were frequent reminders from one to the other to refrain from constantly dwelling on events in the past as they could prove to be catalysts for derailing the train of thoughts. Whereas one party believed strongly in the use of logic, the other had faith only in sentiment. Under such a circumstance, a mutually acceptable outcome was highly improbable. Thus the battle raged on until it was finally interrupted by the ringing of the door bell. Their daughter had returned, only to find the mother eager to vent her frustration on the poor child. Strangely enough, Swasti had apparently anticipated such a reaction from her mother. She let her mother know that she found her mother's behaviour to be predictable. The cold breakfast served the next morning complemented the chilly mood at the table.

It was time for their first born to take driving lessons. The father had learned to drive in India with his friend as the instructor. The friend was more experienced than he, having obtained his driver's license the previous week. It had been a challenge to manage the clutch, the accelerator and the break all at the same time while avoiding jaywalking humans, stray animals, dung from holy cows and large potholes. Satyananda offered to train Swasti. The resistance from the other members of the family caught him by surprise. Although Kalavati had never had experience driving on Indian roads, she was quick to remind him that all that was required from him then was to drive on the left side of the road. The chaotic traffic would take care of the rest. According to her, steering an automatic vehicle in organized traffic was definitely a bigger challenge. Satyananda wondered how she could make such a comparison since she had never driven a stick-shift car. It was eventually decided that Swasti would learn to drive the correct way, by enrolling in a driving school. Would-be drivers were required to master theory before practical lessons commenced. The heavy dose of theory proved to be counterproductive, evoking resentment in the child. Part way through the course she became restless and was ready to quit. The parents counselled patience and were perhaps more relieved than their daughter when the theoretical portion of the course was finally completed paving the way for practical lessons to commence. The structured training provided by driving schools lowers insurance premiums. This is a bait to trap parents and discourage them from passing on faulty driving habits to their children. After a few lessons driving under actual road conditions, Swasti commented that most of the theory that she was compelled to master was actually unnecessary. Towards the end of the course the instructor ruled that the student had not mastered the art of driving. Extra lessons were recommended. When Satyananda challenged the decision, the driving school took the position that the child's inability to learn to drive was in no way a reflection on the competence of the instructor. Satyananda had supplemented the training by assisting Swasti to perfect parallel parking and highway driving skills for several hours over many weekends. All that effort had not resulted in an overall satisfactory outcome. Discontinuing the services of the driving school was not an option. Doing so would annul the promised discount on insurance premiums. Despite all the effort and expenditure, Swasti eventually obtained her driving licence only on her third attempt. Having reached the long awaited milestone, she was now anxious to experiment with her recently acquired skill. Henceforth there would be additional competition for the use of the single car owned by the family. The mother was uncomfortable being in the same car when the daughter was at the wheel. Having suffered back and side seat driving for numerous years, Satyananda was glad to see Kalavati shifting her attention to Swasti. The frequency of calls for caution increased considerably and their pitch was higher than ever before. Strong words were frequently exchanged between the nervous daughter and her paranoid mother. Then one fine day Kalavati announced that they could travel together only when Swasti was in the passenger seat. Keerti had been quietly absorbing the verbal exchanges and learning from her sister's misery. She had also benefitted from Swasti's rebellion that had resulted in the family owning a second car. She was now required to compete for the older car only with her sister who was sympathetic to her needs and hence willing to share. The siblings were united in their resolve to defeat the designs of a common enemy. Nothing could be worse than the mother intervening to settle their disputes! The children had already established proprietary rights on the first car. The siblings would turn to the father for permission to use the second car when both had need for a vehicle at the same time. Among the parents, it was easier to please the father since he asked few questions and placed no conditions for release.

Security in illusions

By nature, Satyananda was a nonconformist and largely immune to societal influence when it did not suit his personal philosophy on life. As he was preparing to embark on his journey to North America, his father had reminded him that those who forget their roots are condemned to be rootless. To him culture was a very important part of life that could not be dispensed with in order to suit changing environments. As well, social status could not be determined on the basis of the country in which one resided. He was disinclined to subscribe to the popular sentiment that non resident Indians deserve a superior social status over those populating the motherland. He was particularly disturbed at the tendency of some friends to paint a gloomy picture of contemporary conditions in India and label it as substandard when compared to life in North America. There was a tendency to focus only on the negative aspects of life back home while promoting only the positive attributes of life in their adopted land. It seemed necessary for some to constantly convince themselves that their decision to desert their motherland was justified. In Satyananda's circle of friends, one gentleman going by the name of Keshav seemed to be ever eager to deride the very traditions which had sustained his survival when migrating from India as a student but had since chosen to jettison. He was particularly harsh when speaking about his younger brother's lifestyle in India. He would often relate his misgivings to Satyananda.

My brother Madhav is a simpleton.
Why?
He is a hopeless idealist. Why does he have to be so traditional?
Why not?
Come on! What is the need to stick to age old customs?

Because they have been tested and proven for centuries?
Seriously! Why can't these Indians be practical?
Who are we to preach to them? We are only hyphenated Indians. They are true Indians.
What do you mean?
They are called Indians, period. We call ourselves Indo-Canadians and they call us NRIs – Non Resident Indians in our presence and Never Returning Indians behind our backs. We should be grateful that they are still willing to accept us.
Madhav is insisting on matching his daughter's horoscope with those of eligible bachelors. I don't know why my innocent niece is putting up with such nonsense.
How old is she?
Only twenty five....Why does he have to marry her off at such a young age?
She is not a child bride Keshav.
I know...but at least she can learn from my daughter.

Keshav's daughter had chosen to live with her boyfriend for several years until she was well past thirty. It was clear to Satyananda that Keshav had no objection to sacrificing the hallowed institution of marriage at the altar of progressive thinking. Apparently, it was imperative to ensure the supremacy of the illusory concept of freedom of choice even if it meant forfeiting time tested traditional wisdom. Little did Keshav realize that his daughter was waiting patiently for her parents to accumulate sufficient savings to pay for a grand wedding ceremony that she had in mind. When his daughter and her companion finally announced their plans to tie the knot, the doting parents were told in no uncertain terms that their role was largely limited to settling the bills for expenses incurred. It was expected that the planning of the event and the selection of invitees would be left entirely to the discretion of the soon to be bride and groom. As a special concession, the parents were allotted a few slots on the list to allow them to invite only very close relatives and friends. Satyananda was unwittingly drawn into the conflict when, at the parent's behest he tried to negotiate with the daughter. Every little plea to expand the list was mercilessly declined even though the parents had agreed to foot the bill. The marriage ceremony was held at a large five star hotel. The event was marked with a brief religious ceremony in the morning and a long reception the same evening. The couple wished to have a brief religious ceremony and had set a rigid standard for the selection of the officiating priest. Priests who believed marriage to be a sacred event refused to agree to an hour long ceremony since they considered the proposal to be an insult to an ancient tradition. A part time certified freelancer who specialized in conducting micro ceremonies was eventually located.

Satyananda observed that the priest commenced the ceremony by mispronouncing sacred *mantras* even as he lit a small fire which spun out of control when he emptied a large can of clarified butter into the *havan kunda*. A number of events occurred in rapid succession thereafter. First, there was general commotion as some guests unaccustomed to wearing traditional Indian dresses made an attempt to contain the fire. In their haste, some tripped over their dresses and almost offered themselves as oblations into a fire that was yet to be sanctified. A potential tragedy was averted thanks to the timely intervention of the alert priest who was by then, on his feet and ready to bolt at short notice. He had placed himself in a strategic position that allowed him to stretch his arms to break the fall of female guests. This action resulted in a shift in his center of gravity. He lost his balance and was in danger of being pulled into the raging fire. Fortunately, years of experience working as a loader at the airport had endowed him with a pair of strong arms and steady feet that permitted him to hold his ground. Next, the fire alarm went on full blast and caused some anxiety and panic among the other residents at the hotel who were now being directed to evacuate the building. The sprinklers were automatically activated and although the fire was extinguished everyone in the room was drenched to the skin. The ceremony came to an abrupt end with uncertainty as to whether or not the bride and groom were eligible to be declared husband and wife. Nonetheless, the priest took credit for having apparently completed the ceremony, a debatable conclusion for which he earned the everlasting gratitude of the couple. It so happened that the bride was rendered unconscious from smoke inhalation and was thus oblivious to the commotion around her. The groom reacted in time to break her fall and head for the exit, to get to which he had to go around the fire carrying her in his arms. This show of chivalry was interpreted by the worldly-wise self-trained priest to be in line with the protocol for sacramental rites performed during a wedding ceremony. He was of the opinion that this could be technically interpreted as a circumambulation of the ritualistic fire by the couple. Not surprisingly, his verdict went unchallenged since potential witnesses were preoccupied with covering themselves in a desperate attempt to preserve their modesty. The priest was rewarded with a generous tip for his kindness in issuing an official marriage certificate. The newly married couple agreed wholeheartedly that the hefty bill for cleaning the mess, presented by the hotel management to the parents, was a small price to pay. Thank goodness they had all emerged from the ordeal unscathed. Indeed their daughter expected Yashoda and Keshav to be grateful to the management for shielding them from the police and attendant legal action. Despite this temporary setback, all was not lost. No doubt the morning had been ruined but the best part of the day was yet to come. Except for the parents no one really cared for a religious ceremony anyways. They should have known better than to compel western educated youngsters to be a party to such mumbo-jumbo. How could any right minded individual disagree that drinking and dancing was the most important part of a respectable wedding ceremony?

The evening programme unfolded exactly as planned. Significantly, the liquor bar was open throughout the evening and into the middle of the night. Once the guests were comfortably seated at the tables assigned to them, they were subjected to a series of long-winded speeches from the best man, the lead bridesmaid, siblings and the parents on both sides. The history of the relationship between the couple was laid bare unreservedly by those whom the couple believed to be their close friends. Each speech was followed by a round of catcalls, polite clapping, loud laughter and tentative pecking of cheeks. The elderly women in particular, took extraordinary care not to disturb the delicate positioning of the undersized dresses that miraculously covered portions of their generous anatomies. It was also essential to ensure that the thick makeup on their weathered faces was not at risk when they dabbed their dry eyes to wipe away imaginary tears. Dinner was finally served along with a heavy dose of entertainment. Not so young girls exhibited their passion for dancing to the tunes of popular *Bollywood* music. Some elderly gentlemen who were still sober enough to be conscious of the proceedings were seen to look away in embarrassment.

Cataract was surely a blessing in such situations. The grand finale of the evening unfolded with the surviving guests gyrating furiously on the dance floor. A few were committed to reducing the spirits in their blood to levels safe enough to avoid a charge for driving under the influence of alcohol. Nonetheless at the end of the celebrations a number of guests who had hovered around the bar throughout the evening could barely stand upright. A few had passed out from excessive consumption and had to be carried away lest the young unruly children trip over them. Indeed, this had been a memorable event!

Later that year, Keshav chose to attend his niece's wedding in India only to return highly disappointed at the turn of events.

> *You know, there was no wedding reception. They could have cut down on the chanting during the wedding ceremony.*
> *So I gather it was a traditional wedding.*
> *I don't understand these guys. No booze? No dancing? How can a wedding be complete without them?*
> *No wedding cake also?*
> *You know what the joker Madhav said when I suggested they have a wedding cake?*
> *Tell me.*
> *He said it is not right to blow out candles. Light is a symbol of auspiciousness. Extinguishing it is a sin. Guests are like gods. We cannot offer them pieces of cake sprayed with saliva.*
> *Anyway, how many guests were there?*
> *Hundreds, What a waste! They should use the cost per plate system for preparing the guest list.*

Never mind that some close friends were callously excluded from Keshav's darling daughter's list of wedding invitees and were no longer on speaking terms with his family. Having married off their daughter, Yashoda and Keshav started taking a keen interest in their son's plans for the future. At 40, Jack had no clue as to how he wished to live the rest of his life. After graduating from high school, he took time off to find himself, only to realize that he was nobody. Prior to that, driving the son to pre-dawn hockey games, junior's routine of hanging out with the boys until the wee hours of the morning and accidents by him while driving intoxicated, had led to premature greying of dad's hairs. Later on, Keshav suffered a heart attack when Jack decided to drop out in the third year of the bachelor of engineering programme in order to switch to creative arts. After trying his luck at various jobs, the enterprising Jack of no trades found gainful employment as a professional poker player. This career move did not surprise the parents since he had shown a talent for gambling very early in his life. His son's career move ensured that the senior worked until he was well past sixty five in order to pay back the enormous debt accumulated by junior. It so happened that under pressure from the doting mother, Keshav had co-signed on the papers for the loan to pay back Jack's gambling debts. It was expected that Jack would find a job and return the money to the bank. The plan had a fatal error. It had made no allowance for the debtor's indifference to the plight of his father. When the son defaulted in his payments, the bank reverted to the father to honour his commitment. For long thereafter, the son continued to survive on the earnings of the father with moral support from the mother.

Meanwhile brother Madhav had retired at age fifty eight and was living a peaceful life in India. Keshav wondered how Madhav could be spending his free time. The answer came in a letter providing vivid details of Madhav's trip to Kashmir to experience snow for the first time in his life.

I had offered to sponsor Madhav's immigration to Canada thirty years ago.
Really? What happened?
He declined. Had he come here, he could have seen tons of snow.
And freezing rain and black ice?
By this time he could have been an expert in operating the snow blower...He does not get enough exercise...He is not physically fit like me.
Keshav, you had a triple bypass some years ago.
Yeah, after that my doc told me I am good for another twenty five years.

He considered himself to be truly blessed to have had this surgery at a well equipped hospital in Canada. Health insurance paid for the bypass surgery and also for the extended stay to treat the exotic mutant bug that he had picked up at the hospital. Yashoda had her hysterectomy experience after the birth of their children via unnecessary caesarean sections.

> *I had offered to present my simpleton brother with the latest lawn mower.*
> *And?*
> *He refused. He said his neighbour's cow was doing it at no cost...When they go out of town the neighbour sleeps in their house to guard it. How can they expose their private lives to strangers?*
> *Trust is very important in that part of the world. You should know that.*
> *Times have changed... you can't trust anyone these days. There are a lot of unemployed people.*
> *Is Madhav still working?*
> *No. He retired last summer. He held a single job throughout his career.*
> *Very steady eh?*
> *Tell me about it.*

On the other hand, Keshav had gained rich experience through several workforce adjustments profiting immensely from severance pay and unemployment insurance benefits. He felt that his hands were cast in gold, considering the number of golden handshakes he had received over the years. Although he held graduate degrees in engineering and management Keshav had worked as a mechanic, a real estate broker, as a financial consultant and for the longest period, as a security guard.

> *Too bad Madhav did not immigrate when he had the chance.*
> *Why so?*
> *Many would be willing to give up an arm and a leg to live in Canada.*

Never mind that a large part of it is buried in snow for several months in a year?
Who cares for quality of life? Standard of living is the only thing that matters.
You mean Madhav has a lesser standard of living than us?
Ofcourse! He does not even own a single car.
But he can ride an elephant. Jokes apart, Is he happy?
I guess so.
Then he is the lucky one.

Sacred circus

Prompted by his pious mother, Satyananda had permitted prayer to play a crucial role in his life. It was more of a routine exercise than a plea for fulfillment of any particular desire. His family resided in a predominantly Christian neighbourhood replete with stone altars at street corners. The faithful would place lighted candles as offerings to the symbolic image of the Holy Cross. Satyananda was often seen praying at these altars on bent knees making the ritualistic sign of the cross. He believed he had created a perfect balance by practicing Hinduism at home and Christianity elsewhere. He loved Hindu festivals and felt previleged to have been born in that ancient faith. He enjoyed watching and listening to his father chanting from the scriptures while offering sweetmeats and fruits to the deities. He would wait patiently for the conclusion of ceremonies in order to receive his share of these wonderful delights. This according to him, was the best part of the ritual. From an early age, Satyananda had been immensely fortunate to have been blessed by numerous spiritually advanced individuals. When as a student, he strayed into the realm of atheism, his actions were perhaps tempered by blessings received through this encounter with divinity during his childhood. Later in life he would regret having spent many years wandering aimlessly in the pursuit of knowledge devoid of spirit. As a child, he was prone to introspection, preferring solitude and often given to conversing with himself. In his teens, he had developed a healthy appetite for reading literature in his spare time which in later life was transformed into a love for books on philosophy. The knowledge imbibed at school and later at university was exclusively tailored towards the secular. Something was missing. He seemed to be constantly in search of that which he could neither guage nor explain, even to himself. This led him to behave unpredictably in certain situations, often interpreted as mood swings by those around him. Although rebellious at times, he was conscious of his boundaries and had unconditional respect for authority when he perceived it to be just. For some reason, he could not tolerate injustice covert or otherwise and was inclined to side with the havenots even under circumstances that could be detrimental to his own interests. This could perhaps be attributed to his middle class upbringing in a neighbourhood that was close to a massive slum. He had witnessed poverty existing in the midst of plenty and blatant disregard by the rich for the misery of the underprevileged. Their plight was perhaps the stimulus for his leftist leanings during early adulthood when he passed through a brief phase of doubt about the very existence of a universal creator.

Satyananda was acutely aware that only a disciplined mind and a strong physique could lead to the development of an allround personality. He had read several books narrating the journeys undertaken by realized souls in their determined quest towards the mastery of the self. This ignited an internal urge in him to follow in their footsteps. However the demands placed on him by terrestrial obligations had to be fulfilled prior to probing into the realm of the transcendental. Once he had a reasonably stable and secure job to attend to the basic needs of his family, he was quick to start the long and arduous process of self discipline. Waking up daily at an early hour he first practised *yoga* and *praanayam* and then permitted himself to dive into meditation for short periods. On a particular morning while in deep meditation, he saw a bright light glowing intensely in his mind's eye. It gradually reduced in size and disappeared after a short while. For a few months thereafter, he went on an emotional roller-coaster ride as he lost control over his mind. He was reduced to being a helpless witness as his mind repeatedly projected a single thought to the exclusion of all others. A callously uttered racist remark by an insensitive colleague played repeatedly in his mind over and over again like a broken record. He spent several sleepless nights trying desperately to create another thought. The demands of a taxing job and the turmoils of raising two very young children were taking its toll on his health. By now he was physically weak, mentally burnt out and very close to a nervous breakdown. He seemed to be spiraling into a state of mental imbalance. He complained of chest pain to his family physician who referred him to a cardiologist. After a series of diagnostic tests at the local heart institute the verdict pointed to a possible cardiac episode. It was then that Satyananda decided to take back control of his life. Through determined effort he overcame the hurdles posed by his erratic mind. After a few months, apart from the occassional nightmare, the mind seemed to have returned to normal. He narrated the sequence of events to a trusted spiritual teacher. The learned sage assured him that only the Lord's grace had protected him from sinking into an irreversible state of madness. Satyananda had read about the effects of accidental and uncontrolled arousal of the dormant *shakti* and was convinced that his symptoms had been very similar to those described in the article. He sensed that he should move forward only with great caution. Spirituality is a vast universe and is largely a subjective experience in consciousness. It is therefore not surprising that an objective assessment of individual progress can seldom be accomplished through precise testing techniques. Nevertheless there is a science associated with the journey that is believed to end in self realization. At what stage in life and under which circumstances should the journey commence is not clearly defined and is subject to one's cicumstances in life often accelerated through inspiration received from realized souls. Satyananda was interested in overcoming his banal urges but his efforts were constantly hindered by the environment in which he lived and worked. Inspired by the life of a living spiritual Master, he voluntarily chose to be a part of His fold. The Master was a spiritual giant in a small physical frame that encapsulated an embodiment of love, patience and fortitude. His presence could captivate and transform die-hard non-believers who may have strayed into the domain of divinity either accidentally or out of sheer curiosity. The faithful believed that nothing happened by chance and that none could hope to be in the divine presence unless the Master wished it so.

Visits to the Guru's ashram in India were always memorable. This was a place of contrasts where displays of various unpleasant emotions competed with spontaneous acts of selfless service and sacrifice. One was exposed to a variety of human expressions and learned practical lessons in patience, fortitude and forbearance. The first few days in the ashram were generally chaotic as devotees had to deal with the trauma of waking up before sunrise and bathing in ice cold water. Health experts often extol the rejuvenating effects of cold water. Undoubtedly that was far from the minds of those contemplating a bath in the wee hours of a cold morning. Satyananda was quick to observe that taking a bath with cold water had an unusual side effect. God's name emerged spontaneously as a cry for mercy from the shivering body even as it effortlessly negotiated the complicated movements of an instantaneously choreographed dance. The bathroom was no place for contemplation as the next customer waited impatiently on the other side of the door. The urge to be externally clean and presentable to the Guru was compelling enough to override any inclination to postpone the misery. Practice they say makes perfect. With each passing day, the pilgrims would perfect this chore to a fine art by reducing the time elapsed between entry and exit from the bathroom. This ashram offered an ideal environment for people of all dispositions. It provided opportunities for meditation and contemplation to the sage, devotion to the pious and equal or more avenues for those inclined towards service. It was surprising that despite being in the immediate presence of the Guru and being well acquainted with His teachings, devotees chose to knowingly litter the sacred premises. The Guru had constantly entreated devotees to be ever alert to opportunities for personal development; to train their minds to remain in the present and refrain from wandering either into the bygone past or the uncertain future. In the presence of the Master the various preoccupations that torment the mind would vanish. There would be no worries about food, clothing or accommodation. Each exhilarating experience of the Guru's physical presence would increase one's anxiety to behold the lustrous physical form again and to regain the experience one more time. The peace that would descend was beyond description. Trips can be memorable for a variety of reasons, some pleasant and others to the contrary. The experiences of devotees were invariably wholesome and fulfilling except for the occasional mistreatment meted out by the volunteers responsible for maintaining order in the ashram. These individuals were inclined to take the law into their own hands in order to enforce their version of discipline. As a deterrent to those who may entertain even a remote desire to bend the rules, they would occasionally make an exhibition of physically lifting and evicting seemingly errant devotees from the prayer hall. Given an opportunity these devotees would perhaps prefer to voluntarily walk to the gate rather than being subjected to such humiliation. The volunteers often worked long hours. Some exhibited telltale signs of sleep deprivation. They could be seen moving around with blood shot eyes, sticks in hand ever ready to pounce on anyone at the slightest provocation. Mothers used them as a means to encourage young children to do their bidding.

Leading national delegations of devotees on visits to the Master's ashram was a major opportunity for office bearers to exhibit their latent talents. On one occasion, on receiving a special invitation from the Master, a delegation of devotees from devotional groups accross Canada visited the ashram. The group comprised a large number of south asians and a few caucasians. Upon arrival at the ashram, the leader of the delegation released an unusual directive. Apparently she was seized with an overwhelming desire to ensure that caucasians received more previleges than the rest of the group. Seating was arranged in a manner that provided them an unobstructed view of the Master when he entered the prayer hall. The others were quick to realize that they were victims of discrimination. A strong protest was lodged imploring the administrative head of the ashram to intervene. Thereupon the Canadian national leader expressed surprise and indignation at what in her opinion was an unacceptable level of intolerance towards foreigners. In her learned opinion such behaviour was highly inappropriate for devotees of the Master. They were reminded that eastern spiritual culture required that guests be treated like gods and since these devotees were guests in India, it behoved others to grant them certain special previleges. This national leader who was otherwise known to be highly opinionated and intolerant of any opposition to her authority, was now putting on a show of pleading for love and tolerance. Very quickly she realized that devotees could be uncompromising on principles and even contemptuous of authority when the stakes are high. This lady was taken to task with a stern reminder that India was equally a foreign country to many dark skinned devotees in the delegation. The Master's teachings on brotherly, sisterly and neighbourly love were permitted to rest in peace as the squabble continued through a major part of the day.The matter was finally resolved when the administrative head of the ashram ruled that previleges could not be based on the colour of one's skin. The remainder of the stay would have been pleasant had the Canadian national leader not repeatedly usurped for herself, the honour of presenting a bouquet to the revered Master on behalf of the Canadian delegation. This task was considered to be an honour reserved only for the most worthy among the devotees. It would have been understandable had the said leader exercised this previlege once, but doing so repeatedly was seen by some as tantamount to an abuse of authority. Permitting another to do the honours on the second and subsequent occasions would have been the honourable thing to do. Leading by example was apparently not one of her strengths. It appeared to many, that in the circles of power selflessness was more a subject of idle conversation than a practical concept. For this individual in particular, practice before precept was clearly an impractical proposition. This leader resigned from her position shortly after the delegation returned to Canada.

A sincere seeker is tormented by many impedements and hurdles. He is required to surmount them all in his quest for the ultimate truth. This may take several life times. Man is a social animal and even in the aspect of spirituality is most comfortable when surrounded by like minded people often referred to as devotees of a particular God or Guru. The fact that these so called devotees may often present the greatest obstacle to one's spiritual progress is a danger that comes with the territory. One should consider oneself very fortunate if one is blessed with fellow devotees who believe in simple living and high thinking. There is an element of challenge in avoiding the circle of hypocracy led by those who consider themselves to be the custodians of the spiritual legacy left behind by the Master. Some individuals chose to annoint themselves with leadership positions and assumed the role of spokespersons for the founder of the movement. Many of these were no better than puppets in the hands of the powerful. Those who preached the Master's teachings the loudest, were often the last to put them into practice. While overtly professing a dislike for rich food, such devotees could be found indulging freely and fearlessly either in the solitude of their homes or at restaurants not frequented by serious devotees. The majority of devotees exhibited a tendency to bring down spiritual conversations to their own level of comfort often steering stimulating philosophical discussions towards mundane issues. After several unsuccesful attempts to keep discussions focused on core spirituality, the true seeker would eventually succumb to the pressure and bow out of the movement. As a result there was a constant tussle between the serious and the casual spiritualists, the latter preferring to admit any and everyone willing to accord a higher status to the kitchen than to the prayer hall. The net outcome was an overemphasis on catering to the needs of the belly at the expense of spiritual health. It did not bode well for a spiritual movement when devotees present in the kitchen outnumbered those in the prayer hall. The populators of the kitchen were often under the mistaken notion that they were rendering a form of service by feeding the hungry. Little did they realize that feeding the already overfed was nothing more than a contribution to the promotion of gluttony. It had nothing to do with rendering selfless service to the needy.

The air in the kitchen of the premises owned by the devotional group was frequently thick with numerous possibilities for conflict. Attempts by certain devotees to impose their will on others was often met with staunch resistance. This would ultimately be resolved through division of territory. Unspoken boundaries were established with devotees choosing to work in their own groups in certain sections of the kitchen. There were frequent debates and disagreements on trivial matters.

Who has cut the vegetables today?
I did. Why?
You have not cut them in the right way.
You mean their size?
No. If you cut them the right way, the juice stays inside.The dish tastes better.
Really?
Who is going to prepare the dish?
Santoshi.
Santoshi make sure that you fry the onions until they are brown.
We are not using onions!
Why not?
This is prasaad. South Indians do not use onions and garlic in prasaad.
Why?
They are Rajasic. We only use Satwick vegetables.
OK but make sure that you add the beans before the egg plant.

> *I have been cooking this dish since I was young. I know how to prepare it.*
> *It was too spicy when you prepared it the last time.*
> *It is meant to be spicy. That is why we serve yogurt with it.*
> *I do not like yogurt with my meal.*
> *Then don't eat the dish also.*
> *But it is prasaad!*
> *Yogurt is also prasaad.*

The politics of expectation was often played out in dramatic detail at meetings which would predictably be inconclusive. Many a times, they would end with a profound statement from someone to the effect that everything takes place in accordance with the will of the Lord. Much time, effort and aggravation could have been avoided if this wisdom had prevailed prior to creating such situations. It would be unwise to expect the Lord to apply His will to inconsequential matters when there are numerous crises demanding His express attention. It could very well be argued that human beings are endowed by Him with the faculty of free will to manage such situations on His behalf. Evidently some previleged humans are free to exercise their wills so long as they could get away with it and invoke the Almighty's intervention when they could not. The Master's teachings on the importance of detachment from the fruits of one's actions were indeed a useful tool to be employed when convenient.

Proprietary rights were claimed by some devotees, on the operation of certain equipment on the premises. The dishwasher in the kitchen and the sound system in the prayer hall being the most popular among them. Some were known to drive away those who were already performing the task of washing dishes after the devotees had partaken of the meal. Incredible as it may seem to be, this mundane task had its rewards. Since the dishwasher was placed in a highly visible part of the kitchen, the relatively simple task of loading plates, bowls and spoons into a dishwasher was quickly rewarded by recognition from the devoted diners. The more strenuous efforts of others scrubbing oversized utensils at the back of the kitchen went largely unnoticed. Visibility was indeed rewarding to those who sought recognition but a curse to those who wished to remain annonymous. In this spiritual arena it was an unspoken rule that recognition would be disproportionate to the effort. It was also observed that those who worked the hardest were inclined to advertise their contributions the least. The fruits of their labour was offered unconditionally by them in the interest of the larger good. The operation of the sound system was another story. There were frequent complaints and counter complaints for and against the operator. Apparently he was known to modulate the system to enhance the quality of performance of his favourites while at the same time brilliantly orchestrating disturbances when the unfavoured held the microphone.

In theory, weekly spiritual discussion forums were meant to encourage collective learning through exchange of knowledge on spiritual matters. However this fertile ground was exploited by some assertive devotees to implant their misguided theories in gullible minds. Faced with a captive audience ever eager to please, such devotees succumbed to the temptation of pontificating on the Master's teachings. They had mastered some catchy phrases from numerous discourses delivered by the Master over the years. These were employed liberally to cloak a shallow understanding of the profound subject matter. It was important to appear intelligent and well informed. There were contradictions galore. The same arguments could be advanced to affirm the opinions of some or to negate those of others. As per the rules, proceedings were required to be summarized and read out to the congregation. This was seldom the practice. The facilitator would prepare a summary prior to convening the discussion forum thereby saving himself the trouble of taking down notes. Thus the summary that was read out to the congregation would have very little in common with the discussions. To be fair, the facilitator could not be faulted as it was seldom possible to derive logical conclusions when certain vociferous participants were in full cry. Gradually the numbers dwindled as participants complained about lack of focus and purpose and the forum eventually died a natural death. The domineering individuals then shifted their attention to the practice sessions for devotional singing. It was now the turn of the participants of this group to be enlightened by the wisdom of these stalwarts. The foundation of the movement rested on devotional singing, the quality of which was maintained through a rigidly enforced protocol. While keeping the skeletal structure unchanged, the rules of engagement were subject to modification. The prefect solution seemed to be perennially out of reach. Singers who met stringent criteria established by a group of experts, would lead the chorus. On any given day success or failure of the programme was determined by the quality of the devotional singing. Devotees were known to be merciless in their criticism of singers whose performance failed to meet their expectations. An unwritten hierarchy had been established among chosen singers based on number of years of experience and quality of delivery. There was an element of competition among equals. They were prone to keeping tabs on each other. Only the fit survived. The faint-hearted fell by the wayside hesitant to rise again. Some lead singers believed they had exclusive monopoly over a selection of signature songs in their repertoire. They frowned upon any attempts by others to reproduce, mimic or alter their renditions, particularly when these received wide acclaim from appreciative devotees. Accomplished singers were routinely at loggerheads with the coordinator over the number of songs alloted to them. Not surprisingly, seniority could often override talent. Yet, the overall quality of singing was miraculously maintained at a high level.

Children of various ages were enrolled in a structured programme that focused on imparting human values. A detailed cirriculum was widely distributed to the parents but rarely read and understood by them. During speech and debate competitions some children were known to regurgitate information downloaded from the internet with the full knowledge and consent of their parents. There was concern among teachers that plagiarism was being encouraged, albeit unintentionally. The apologists were quick to seek shelter under a particular requirement in the curriculum that spoke to a need for creating opportunities for encouraging public speaking skills among children. In their collective opinion the collateral damage to ethics could be condoned in the larger interest of keeping the children engaged in productive activities. For many parents, the Sunday school was primarily a medium for exhibiting their childrens' talent for acting. Plays on various themes were enacted at least once every year. To the less informed, this was explained away as a forum for creating opportunities for role play, a curricular requirement. It was not uncommon to witness doting mothers putting forth creative arguments when they believed that their children were not assigned important roles. According to some, fairness had been unjustly compromised in favour of discipline when roles were alloted based on attendance and not on talent. The most coveted roles were reserved for those who were punctual and had a good record of attendance throughout the year. Ability to act was not a criterion since prerecorded dialogues were played even as the actors went through the physical motions on stage. The process had been perfected over a number of years and was therefore very efficient. Theoretically, attendance should have improved as a consequence but quite to the contrary, there was little or no competition. The children exhibited visible signs of boredom during auditions and rehearsals. That which was considered a failure by the adults was apparently seen as a blessing by the children as they did not have to work as hard as those playing lead roles. Attendance at Sunday school would drop drastically after the play had been finally enacted on stage in front of an audience composed largely of parents and grandparents who had high stakes in its success. When asked to explain the absence of their children from regular Sunday school after the annual play had been staged, parents were quick to advance flimsy excuses in their own defence. Attempts to debar truant children and their parents were met with stiff resistance from some teachers. They were interested more in retaining the names of the children in the register than in imparting the virtues of discipline. Apparently, numbers were an indicator of the popularity of the Sunday school. The situation had been allowed to progressively deteriorate over the years by repeatedly condoning such absenteeism. Indeed all students enrolled on the register received the customary certificates of completion, some for full attendence and others for mere participation. It was essential to keep everyone happy in order to ensure that they returned the following year. These certificates were cast aside in some corner of the child's bedroom until they would eventually make their way into recycling bins. Traditionally, students from the graduating class were provided with an opportunity to express their thoughts on how they had benefited from the many years invested by them in Sunday school. Typically their responses showed the teachers and parents in favourable light. These young adults had nothing to loose and much to gain by keeping their elders happy. By choosing their words carefully they were able to please those teachers who derived satisfaction in considering these words of gratitude as testimonials for their competence. These valedictory speeches were the only prevalent yardstick for measuring the efficacy and impact of the knowledge imparted. This was also employed as a benchmark for assessing teaching skills. The majority of parents did not profess any interest in finding out what their children were learning in these classes. They were content to leave their children in a secure location while they utilized the time to attend to other business. Hence, there was a general unwillingness to rock the boat either among the parents, the teachers or the taught.

A strategist in the national think tank came up with the brilliant idea of hosting an annual run for promoting *nonviolence*. This was considered a practical means of raising the profile of the movement. The idea was simple yet pregnant with possibilities, considering that the intent was to attract new members to the fold. Members of devotional groups across the country were expected to run a predetermined course holding placards extolling the virtues of practicing nonviolence. Participants were required to take a solemn pledge to uphold the principles of nonviolence in their daily lives. In subsequent years, this activity was elevated to the status of a marathon. High profile politicians were invited to deliver motivational speeches at the event. Not long thereafter, the event was transformed into a grand spectacle with the introduction of partnership with private sponsors whose names, logos and mandates were displayed during the run. Typically banners and floats would advertise a list of sponsors in font sizes commensurate with their contributions. There was no expectation that the partners profess allegiance to the spiritual movement. Gradually control of the event shifted to the partners who had by then organized themselves into a powerful conglomerate. Sentiments of the movement that were drivers for the event in the formative years were initially trampled upon and later cast aside in the haste to make the event a profitable venture. It was only a matter of time before differences in philosophies came to the fore. There ensued a prolonged tussle for control over the marathon and the dispute was eventually dragged to the courts. Even as the learned judges were deliberating on the issue of ownership, at the next marathon strong unprintable words were exchanged between the feuding groups culminating in physical altercations. Ironically, the original intent of the organizers to seek publicity for the movement was fulfilled when it was widely covered in the media under the heading: “Spirited display by spiritualists”. The marathon was now transformed into a battleground. The weak had no choice but to yield to the strong when banners were snatched away from them. Although only the meek were expected to inherit the marathon, the bold had now taken undisputed control over the event. In response to such unprovoked acts of aggression, the following year, there were an abundance of signs imploring participants to maintain *peace*. The overload of misinformation being freely circulated by the warring factions without let or hindrance resulted in additions to the placard family the following year. *Truth* and *right conduct* were now introduced as subtle appeals to those responsible for spreading rumours and semi-truths. In due course a particularly vocal group intent on promoting their brand of liberal thinking decided to exploit this opportunity to make their presence felt. Displaying suggestive caricatures on their jerseys proclaiming the virtue of *love*, the couples were seen to pause at regular intervals during the course of the marathon in order to openly display intimacy amongst each other. This side show was often greeted with a volley of cat calls and invectives which would prompt some concerned mothers to cover the ears of their young and impressionable children. What had begun as an innocent and perhaps a naive attempt to promote a desirable virtue had now been transformed into a forum for expressing the opposite sentiment. Its scope had been inadvertently broadened to include a spectrum of human values such as *truth, right conduct, peace, love* and *nonviolence*. The prominence accorded to them in aerial displays did not translate into action on the ground. Verbal and physical violence became a predictable feature of this marathon. Abuse that originated in thought was freely expressed in word and followed through in deed. Water bottles and cans of soda were tossed around, some acting as potent missiles when they landed on delicate parts of the human anatomy. Participation declined sharply when rumours were circulated that certain anarchist groups were planning to launch acid bombs disguised as water bottles. In the midst of this confusion came word that the judges of the court had finally delivered a unanimous verdict on the disputed event. By this time neither of the parties involved in the litigation were willing to assume ownership of the marathon. It was a great relief to both sides on learning that the learned members of the judiciary had recommended that the event be discontinued since it served no useful purpose. Thus the marathon for nonviolence had run its unintended course starting from nothing and ending in naught. Those individuals who had previously competed aggressively to be in the limelight were all of a sudden, conspicuous by their absence. A terse statement in the movement's newsletter announced that in deference to the wishes of the court, the marathon had been withdrawn from the list of annual events.

Rise of a spiritual orphan

Apparently, in the modern world even pious souls are not exempt from competition. Threatened by the potential erosion of their membership on account of the growing popularity of the Master, some groups began a vicious campaign to malign Him. On His part, the Master was seemingly unaffected by the adverse publicity, even going to the extent of urging his followers to refrain from reacting to any provocation. Nevertheless, as a result of sustained efforts by such groups, a significant number of devotees in some western countries deserted the movement. Taking this to be a sign of the decline of the Master's influence, those who were in the fold for the wrong reasons were quick to head for the door. Highly inflammatory articles were posted on the internet by former devotees. The media worked overtime to create and disseminate nonexistent news about alleged improprieties on the part of the Master. In the midst of all this, the movement saw the rise of a few evangelists. These devotees claimed to have had the privilege of being in close proximity with the Master. They were placed on a high pedestal and treated by the faithful with the utmost respect and adoration bordering on hero worship. They toured the world to promote their version of the Master's teachings, a task for which they claimed to have received express sanction from the Master. One such devotee took to draping himself in a saffron robe imitating the Master's attire while claiming to be speaking for and on His behalf. Some of those who were granted the privilege of a private audience chose to publish their conversations with the Master. Unfortunately the methods prescribed by the Master for the exclusive benefit of these authors were erroneously interpreted by many as directives from the Guru for the spiritual progress of the masses. They were used to promote the mistaken notion that the Master was in favour of having one set of standards for devotees residing in

India and another for those living in western countries. This was entirely contrary to the universality of the *dharma* propagated by the Master.

The revered Master had been ailing for some time. His frail body seemed to shrink each passing year. Yet the Master stuck to a punishing daily routine that began at sunrise and ended at a late hour every day of the week. During the final days, the faithful kept vigil with simultaneous prayer sessions at devotional groups worldwide. When news broke, there was widespread grief at the Master's demise. Satyananda was devastated. A life without the physical presence of his Guru seemed unbearable. For many days thereafter, tears would flow spontaneously from his eyes as he sat in front of a life-sized picture of the Master reminiscing on the past. Recovery was gradual and painful. The winds of change blowing across the movement carried away the fragrance of days bygone. The exodus from the North American segment of the movement commenced soon after the revered Guru gave up his mortal coils. Over a period of time some high level office bearers who had held responsible positions in the movement for several years stepped down on one pretext or the other. Others who had build a voluntary career out of promoting the illusion of an apparent lack of unity among devotees were no longer in demand. These were masters at doublespeak adept in the art of dodging searching questions from sincere devotees by cloaking their answers in unintelligible spiritual jargon. Devotees were now openly critical of speakers who compensated for their lack of ability to deliver clear spiritual messages with theatrical antics bordering on the ludicrous. Departing from previous custom that demanded unquestioned obedience to authority, there was now a marked unwillingness to devote precious time and energy to suffer lectures that lacked focus. As a consequence of such indifference, those who had hitherto enjoyed a favoured status on the speakers' circuit, were compelled to seek favourable pastures outside the movement. When they departed, these high profile individuals advanced innovative arguments to justify their defection to other spiritual movements. According to them, spiritually advanced souls such as themselves were perfectly entitled to seek guidance elsewhere in pursuit of knowledge. This, in their opinions, was perfectly aligned with the Master's advice to reach out, expand and experience the underlying unity in diversity. Strangely enough, in order to keep the flock together the very same individuals had argued to the contrary during their tenure in leadership positions in the movement. Other spiritual Masters were prohibited from addressing congregations on the pretext that their preachings could potentially confuse committed devotees. In essence, the ability of the average devotee to discriminate between right and wrong was being undermined by those who wished to think on their behalf. Those left behind in the rush for the exit felt that the departure of such shallow devotees was indeed a sign of the Lord's grace upon followers who continued to be faithful to the memory of their Guru. Indeed, the relevance of an organized movement that placed undue reliance on administrators to provide spiritual direction, was now being brought into question. Tragically, armchair philosophers had stepped into the shoes of a realized Master.

At this critical juncture, Satyananda was invited to lead the devotional group of which he had been a longstanding member. Lessons learned over the years were prompting him to decline this offer. Yet he believed that this was a sign from his departed Guru to serve the congregation to the best of his ability. Accepting the responsibility, he set to work in earnest. In order to develop a direction tailored to their needs he consulted a number of devotees on their expectations. These interactions confirmed his belief that congregational members were mature and perfectly capable of making their own judgements in spiritual matters. Acting on their feedback, Satyananda doggedly promoted spiritual activities that were frowned upon by some influencial devotees who were intent on ensuring that eastern cultural and philosophical practices did not take firm roots in their midst. According to them spiritual activities undertaken by devotional groups in the west should reflect the local culture. They were strongly opposed to time-tested eastern spiritual practices. Chanting from ancient scriptures was discouraged despite the fact that it was a daily feature in the Master's ashram in India. To them it was inconsequential that the sentiments of the majority were being crushed in order to feed the illusion that potential western devotees of the future might be uncomfortable with such practices. From discourses delivered over the years, it was clear that the Master had no intention of establishing diverse spiritual sub-cultures in different parts of the world. Satyananda had nothing to do with the politics within the movement. He believed in learning directly from the Master's teachings without the intervention of intermediaries. He was conscious of a marked shift in position with regard to devotional activities, after the demise of the Guru. Spiritual practices to which the devotees had been hitherto accustomed were now deemed to be unsuited to western culture. A new paradigm for spiritual conduct was being aggressively promoted. Directives percolating down from the top appeared to be in direct conflict with the Guru's teachings which were essentially based on ancient wisdom or *dharma*. On numerous occasions, the Master had expressed His intent to spread the universal principles worldwide. The Master's teachings on *dharma* were being now sacrificed in the haste to project an all inclusive image for the movement. The Master had taught that the principles of ancient *dharma* went beyond the narrow confines placed by cultural and geographical limitations in order to embrace everything in creation under the fatherhood of God. There was no scope for excluding anyone from seeking shelter under such a liberal overarching umbrella. Contrary to the Master's wishes, there were general inconsistencies in the spiritual activities conducted at devotional groups across North America. Some groups preferred to accord a higher value to their interpretation of ethics than to the Master's teachings on *dharma*. A few devotional groups explicitly prohibited the use of the Master's name and the display of His pictures on the premises. Those accustomed to meditating on the Master's form were quick to take offense.

Discipline among children and adults alike was in rapid decline. Erring adults did not take kindly to frequent appeals from Satyananda to maintain discipline and silence in the prayer hall when spiritual sessions were in progress. These individuals were largely disinterested in performing any tasks that required physical exertion. Circumventing spiritual programmes, they would arrive in time for food served at the end of certain special programmes and depart as soon as their objective was realized. A few would even take the opportunity to gossip after the meals were partaken thus delaying the closing of services. Some parents would make no attempt to control their young children from running in the dining hall and creating disturbance as they negotiated the tables and chairs. In the prayer hall a few children would take the initiative to roll around on the carpet and would frequently leave and re-enter the hall while their parents watched unconcerned. Sadly, the assembly had been reduced to the level of a social club disguised as a spiritual group. A few powerful feathers were ruffled when Satyananda chose to first arrest and then reverse these undesirable trends. Anonymous letters were received by the national leader accusing Satyananda of arrogance, high handedness and misuse of power. A congregational meeting was convened to discuss the matter. A record number of members turned up at this meeting, many among them were devotees who had previously never shown any interest in participating in spiritual initiatives. They were there to witness the drama. The interrogation began in earnest.

> *The president is promoting an outdated concept of spirituality.*
> *I am only an instrument for promoting the teachings of the Master. Spirituality is perennial,it cannot be dated or outdated. It has always existed and will continue to exist for eternity.*
> *Your methods for imposing discipline may be alright for India but not for Canada.*
> *I believe I have discharged my duties to the best of my abilities. I know of no other better method. Since in this matter you seem to be more knowledgeable than I, I am open to some suggestions from you.*

Hearing this, several members stood up to voice their opinions. Finally, the person who was able to shout the loudest prevailed over the others.

> *You could speak softly and lovingly.*
> *You are merely quoting the Master. I did try this. Initially, I tried to appeal.... to reason ....to convince. I even had youth carrying signs urging devotees to maintain silence in the prayer hall but to no avail. I had to resort to stronger measures.*
> *Can you explain what you did?*
> *I personally asked some children who were rolling on the floor to sit erect and be quiet.*
> *Did you use strong language?*
> *I do not recall using strong language but I may have used an assertive tone.*

Again some devotees rose to their feet to challenge Satyananda.

> *You are trying to run a military style operation. It is damaging the self esteem of our children. No one should interefere. They have the right to freedom of expression.*
> *Are you saying that rolling on the floor is self expression?*
> *Yes. This is a public place and they should be free to express themselves in whatever way they wish to do so.*
> *This is a temple of learning, not an ordinary public place. Everyone is expected to follow the code of conduct provided by our Master. This is clearly displayed in the hall outside.*
> *The children cannot be expected to understand such complex matters.*
> *Then the parents should control them.*
> *Silence*

From the manner in which individuals were coming forward to support each other's points of view, it was clear to Satyananda that a carefully rehearsed script was unfolding before him. This was no better than an annual shareholder meeting in which the management was taken to task for turning in unsatisfactory results. Nobody seemed to care that an unpaid volunteer was being chastized for doing the right thing.

> *Our children are refusing to come. They do not like your methods. You should apologize.*
> *No one is forcing you to bring your children here. It is entirely your decision. We do not charge any fees. It is a previlege to be here. It is not a right.*
> *Are you suggesting that we should not be coming here?*
> *I am not suggesting anything. I am merely making a statement of fact. You may choose to interpret it the way you want to.*
> *We can all sense your arrogance.*
> *I take my duties very seriously.*
> *We take the trouble to bring our children here. You should be grateful*

> *You bring your children here to learn about human values. Discipline is the foundation for the learning process.*

Many who had supported his methods in private chose to remain silent during the entire proceedings anxious to be in the good books of those who may take control in the future. Looking directly at these individuals he let it be known that he had done nothing wrong and therefore was under no compulsion to offer an apology to anyone. There were more accusations but Satyananda was no longer in a mood to respond. The time had come to lay the matter to rest. Rather than trying to contain the fury of the tempest, the wise course of action would be to abandon this rudderless ship. That night the Master appeared in his dream with a broad smile and His right hand raised in blessing. He woke up the next morning with a feeling of deep fulfillment. A clear path seemed to have emerged with the Master's seal of approval. He had taken a principled stand and it was now time to depart with dignity rather than compromise his commitment to his Guru's teachings. The next day, he stood before the congregation for the last time. The silence was deafening as he surveyed the membership. They sensed that he was poised to make an important announcement. Those who had spoken out the previous day expected to hear an apology. They were throwing knowing glances at each other in anticipation of victory.

> *I stand before you to make a final announcement. I have handed in my resignation and have asked to be relieved of my responsibilities with immediate effect. I consider the length of my service as a humble token of gratitude for the spiritual wealth received from my Guru. To Him and only to Him I owe everything. As for the rest, the sheet is balanced. I owe nothing to anybody and nobody owes me anything. Neither gratitude nor an apology. What has taken place yesterday is an indication of what is to come in the future. This will certainly discourage sincere devotees from accepting positions of authority. I have been labelled as an unfit leader by a few with the power to influence many. Regrettably, the majority among you chose to remain silent while I was being taken to task. I have chosen to resign on account of their silence. I am*

> *reminded of our Master's very famous saying: Silence is the language of spiritual seekers. Alas! these devotees have chosen to apply their Guru's teaching at a wrong time and place. These devotees had put sustained pressure on me to improve discipline and had even expressed their appreciation of my methods in private. I tried to do the right thing without caring for my own popularity since I truly believe that those who choose to follow the dictates of their conscience have nothing to fear. I leave it to my Guru to set the path forward. He is watching over me and will surely lead me to my true goal.*

There was pin drop silence in the hall, as Satyananda calmly walked out of the room. He felt elated as if relieved of a heavy burden.

With a fulfilling professional career and numerous laurels behind him, Satyananda was now contemplating retirement. Lessons learned the hard way had convinced him that the nature of humans is alike irrespective of the country in which they choose to reside. Experience had taught him that greed, corruption and exploitation are universal human character traits that co-exist with charity, honesty and selflessness varying only in the degree of manifestation of their symptoms. He had not failed to note that whereas there is tremendous competition for positions that require little effort but fetch quick recognition, there is little interest in those that demand diligence and hard work. Using transparency and consultation as legitimate reasons for networking, birds of a feather had found a valid excuse to flock together while employing collective wisdom to mask individual ignorance. Satyananda had never wished to rise to the top by standing on the shoulders of others around him. He had advanced only through fair competition at every step in his career path. He felt there was nothing more for him to attain in worldly matters. Providence had been kind to him. It was time for the wave to think about merging back into the ocean from which it had emerged. Looking back on his life, he could find little from the past that he would have liked to change. His children had once wished to know the reason for his decision to immigrate to Canada. At that time, he had claimed that momentary insanity had driven him to desert his beloved native land to seek greener pastures abroad. The land of the gods continued to beckon him when he was away, intrigued him when he was there and enticed him afresh when he returned back to Canada. He had lived the Indian dream all these years, albeit in Canada. With a devoted Indian wife, he resided in a home furnished with artefacts imported from India, recited his *mantras* regularly and ate three Indian meals a day. A typical Sunday evening would end with the family watching the latest *Bollywood* movies on DVD.

A long time had elapsed since he had first learned to play chess from his father. Throughout his happily married life, he had time only to test his skills on the domestic checkerboard. It had been a constant struggle to maintain his status as the king of his castle while trying not to be a pawn in the hands of his queen. He had taken pains to avoid any straws of indiscretions that could have potentially broken the camel's back. Such a behavior would have certainly prompted his better half to label him as a stale mate. His game plan had always been to make sensible moves to hold his horses from self destruction while covertly striving to keep his partner in check even as he made an open show of resigning himself to his fate. Simple living and simple thinking was the motto on which he had based his life. Even so, his health did not always cooperate. He was frequently tormented by arthritic pain and often spent sleepless nights entertaining thoughts of possible health issues that might hinder his return to his beloved motherland. He feared that destiny would interfere in his quest to complete the circle by denying him the opportunity to end his life cycle in the country of his birth. He was now unduly concerned with the place of death that would be cited on his obituary. Henceforth, the misfit would be preoccupied more with death than with living.

Printed in the United States
By Bookmasters